SUSPICION

Returning a little after five, Marta asked, "What's that glass all over the rug in front of the fireplace?"

"I was toasting my retrieved wife, in the Russian fashion," Harley said. The suppressed violence in his voice gave her pause.

"Why hasn't Mrs. Nairn cleaned it up?"

"For the first time in months, the housekeeper has fled this happy home for a weekend elsewhere. She took exception to a request of mine that she put rat poison in your after-dinner Brie."

"Oh, Harley, for God's sake."

Talking wildly, grotesquely, wasn't new to him; he liked to play with the language, sometimes very darkly.

But the overt threat with its hard edge of laughter, the broken glass—he must have thrown it with all his strength, he must have been consumed with rage— bothered her as she went up the stairs to bathe and change.

He wouldn't . . . *do* anything to her, would he?

WELCOME TO THE GRAVE
MARY McMULLEN

JOVE BOOKS, NEW YORK

This Jove book contains the complete
text of the original hardcover edition.
It has been completely reset in a typeface
designed for easy reading, and was printed
from new film.

WELCOME TO THE GRAVE

A Jove Book / published by arrangement with
Doubleday, a division of Bantam
Doubleday Dell Publishing Group, Inc.

PRINTING HISTORY
Doubleday edition published 1979
Jove edition / May 1989

ISBN: 0-515-10011-0

Jove Books are published by The Berkley Publishing Group,
200 Madison Avenue, New York, New York 10016.
The name ''JOVE'' and the ''J'' logo
are trademarks belonging to Jove Publications, Inc.

PRINTED IN THE UNITED STATES OF AMERICA

10 9 8 7 6 5 4 3 2 1

To Alton

ONE

It had been a perfectly splendid morning in April until twenty-seven minutes after eleven.

Chapter Five was going well. The typewriter seemed to be doing the inventing for him and he was hard put to keep up with it, long strong square-tipped fingers flying. He was in the middle of what he considered a hilarious sex scene and hardly knowing it he laughed out loud, his shoulders shaking.

His workroom-library was big and comfortably shadowy, facing west toward a rising meadow decked with apple trees and dandelions; he disliked the morning dazzle of sun in his face. A half-full pot of powerful coffee was waiting on its hot plate to stoke his cup. He found that in his excitement with his scene he had two cigarettes going, in the big crystal ashtray, and laughed again and crushed one out.

He was vaguely aware of the fact that it was a beautiful day. The air flowing in from the west windows was like cool fresh water on his skin. A bird sang in a branch nearby, perhaps a robin; he was no good at birds. "Shut the bloody hell *up!*" he shouted merrily, and raced to keep pace with his typewriter.

For five days a week, his routine was unvarying. Up at seven; the kitchen was all his, as Mrs. Nairn never entered it until seven-thirty. Freshly squeezed orange juice waiting for him in the refrigerator, two pieces of toast, and then the eager dive with his first cup of coffee into the workroom. He stayed there, composing, striding, occasionally stretching himself on the leather sofa to think furiously and often aloud, until two o'clock. Mrs. Nairn had at first been startled by the voice

1

behind the closed door, the laughter, the occasional shouted blasphemy, but after a short time she got used to it.

Work hours over, he would surface and emerge, sometimes shaking himself in a bewildered way, like a dog, as he returned to the other world; he was never quite sure which was the real one. He mixed and drank two icy martinis, was served a light lunch by Mrs. Nairn in the dining room, took a two-hour nap and a four-mile walk, and then launched himself with gusto into the festive hours and the business of having a good time, alone or in company.

It was an iron rule that he was under no circumstances to be interrupted at work. "No phone calls, Mrs. Nairn, not even if it's Jesus Christ on the line. If the house is burning down, tell the fire department but don't tell *me*."

As he got up to fill his coffee cup, there was a light knock at the door.

"Go away," he called, plunging into the middle of a dangling sentence. Puzzling, the knock, though. It couldn't be Mrs. Nairn, and it couldn't be that kid, who was so nearly invisible that most of the time he forgot about her existence. Maybe somebody trying to deliver something or wanting to read a meter. Some mornings, Mrs. Nairn shopped, always turning off the telephone when she left the house.

An impossible thing happened. The door, to which his back was turned, was opened, he heard the quiet creak it always made. His swivel chair whirled in outrage.

His wife Marta came over to him and said, "Hello, Harley."

Thunderstruck, he shot to his feet. In a bewildered way, he asked, stammering a little, "W-what are you— Are you passing through and stopped to say hello or something?" His own words fell ridiculously on his ears. Instinctively, he backed a few feet away from her. His voice changed. "Because if that's the case I think you have one hell of a nerve."

Marta had left him two years ago. It couldn't exactly be called running away, with the man, what was his name? Mandarino?—yes. She had gone about it in a composed and efficient way, while he was immured in work. Packed two suitcases with her best and newest clothes. Left the bed neatly made,

the bathroom immaculate. Written him a note which he found
under the little gold clock on his dresser.

> Dear Harley, I'm off with my Chris. We love and
> need each other. I'm sorry, but we must be together.
> I've taken nothing but clothes and the contents of my
> own checking account. As you know, he's well able to
> take care of me financially. Good luck with your life and
> your work always, and a, believe it, fond goodbye,
>
> Marta

He hadn't heard from her or of her since. After the first
storm of rage—mainly wounded pride; he'd been in the middle
of one of his own numerous affairs—he began the process of
dismissing her, erasing her, and she was now, to him, a stranger.

She was tallish and solidly fleshed, suggesting a strong yet
pillowy body without any running to fat. She had a thick smooth
columnar neck and a rounded face, Renoir-like in coloring,
rose and cream. Her eyes were round and china blue, her golden
hair arranged in a heavy braided chignon at the back of her
head. There was a quality of solid stillness about her. She still
had it. And on close examination, lines that hadn't been there
before, a few, around her eyes and mouth. The never-slim
waist a little more ample. Yes, solid. "Trying to stop Marta
from doing what she wants," he once said, "is like barring
the way of a whale or a nuclear submarine."

Standing in the center of the Chinese rug, "No, I didn't stop
to say hello, Harley," she said. "I'm back for good."

The words exploded somewhere under his rib cage. Voice
gathering volume, he said, "Get out of this room, get out of
this house, there's no place in it for you for sixty seconds."
Smacked pride briefly reasserted itself. "This is no goddamned
Thirties' play, you're over, you're finished." He threw back
his head and laughed with a glee that sounded even to him a
little wild. "What happened, did *he* leave *you* flat? If you're
looking for a handout, forget it."

Calmly, she said, "I'm still married to you. You never
divorced me, there would have been papers and things."

Months back, Jill had said to him, "Haven't you got around to divorcing that woman *yet?* Has it ever occurred to you that if you were in a car crash or something she'd get every penny you own?"

"Good idea, I'll change my will," which he hadn't pursued. Legal matters bored him; which was his own excuse to himself for not having bothered to institute divorce proceedings. He only vaguely suspected his real reason: not liking to inform the watching and listening world that his wife had left him.

"You must," shouting now, "be mad. Absolutely stark staring out-of-your-skull mad. Or is this some kind of joke? It must be some kind of game of yours. If I thought you were serious, you defecting runaway bitch—"

His hand closed on a heavy round crystal paperweight on his desk. He was very much a threatening figure. He was a tall man, with big protuberant blue eyes, fresh fair skin which when he was excited or angry turned red and then a dangerous puce. His large shapely head was completely bald. John McIndoe, his agent, said of him, "Harley has a fine head of scalp," and, "He looks like—his face, I mean—a cross between a Kewpie doll and a gorilla." The great round forehead seemed to go up and up before it met that place where a hairline would have started. He projected always an enormous zest, vitality, absorption in himself, and when emotion swept him he became somehow larger than life.

Marta studied his purpling skin color, the blue fury of the bulging eyes. "You'll give yourself a heart attack, Harley. May I have some coffee? I've been hours on trains and buses."

She had rehearsed this scene on the bus from Bridgeport to Mute. So far it was going according to her mental script. Let him rant, rage, get it out of his system, exhaust himself, before matters of plain common sense were quietly gone into.

Buses were an unusual form of transportation for her. Until six months ago, hers had been a life of taxis, private cars, and jet planes.

In early November, Christoforo Mandarino had left her. That is, he called her from Rome, where he had gone to buy pictures for his gallery in Charleston, South Carolina, and told her that, sorry, darling, they were over, he had decided on an extended stay and had taken an apartment in a palace owned by a contessa who might, with persuasion, marry him.

He'd ask her to stay on and run the Charleston gallery, he said, except that he knew humdrum business matters bored her, and in any case a clean break would be healthier, happier, for both of them.

She packed her clothes, cleaned out her second bank account in two years, left the handsome piazzaed white house, with its fragrant garden, on Meeting Street, and went to live with Kenneth Praloe, an artist who had long since wagged beckoning fingers at her.

This alliance had lasted for four months. He drank a great deal, was sullen and abusive when his work wasn't going well, and worst of all he was broke most of the time, relying heavily on her own dwindling funds. One night she refused him a thousand dollars and he struck her and knocked her halfway across his studio.

She took a bus to New York and after a week found a job selling cosmetics at Elizabeth Arden. She had never before in her life done a day's work for pay. Her feet hurt terribly and she disliked waiting on other women. How rude, how demanding was the world on the other side of the counter.

It was the dentist who was the unknowing catalyst. She had a persistent toothache and Ann Tree, a friend at whose apartment she was staying for the time being, sent her to her man. A long examination in expensive-looking offices, X rays, and then what the receptionist described, making the next appointment, as a conference.

At the conference, the dentist outlined the absolutely necessary work to be done on her mouth, pointing with a gold pen to various places on the hideous grinning X rays. He talked of crowns and bridges and root canals. "Don't be misled by how well you teeth *look,* this is what's happening underneath, and went on to gums and bone. The work would cost in total $1,250.

What first suggested itself was: Have it done and just don't pay him. But then he might take her into court. She said she'd think about it, and went away with her tooth still aching. In two days she got a bill for $100 for the examination and analysis.

She was forty-two. She looked across a frightening chasm to the cliff face of fifty. There would always be another man, wouldn't there? and after him . . .

My God, what if I get *sick?*

What's going to happen when Ann gets tired of my company and I have to find an apartment and pay the rent? And clean it, do things with mops and vacuum? And push a cart around the supermarket?

And that ghastly job at Arden, she hadn't the will or the knack for unloading all kinds of bottles and jars on a customer who had merely asked for eye cream.

Her indulgent father was dead. Her mother had money but was mean with it. When Marta had arrived nearly penniless in New York she had called up and asked for a loan and been told her mother could spare fifty dollars, but beyond that her funds were absolutely tied *up,* darling, tighter than a drum.

Dentists. Illnesses. How many men swarmed around you at fifty, even though you didn't look anywhere near your age?

She quit her job and again packed her bags—the expensive Guccis now showing signs of a wandering unlocated life. This time there was no bank account to close out. She took a train from New York to Bridgeport, and there she boarded the bus to Mute, Connecticut.

"No, I didn't stop to say hello, Harley, I'm back for good."

In the big square sunny kitchen filled with the sounds and the rainbow sparkles of the waterfall, ten-year-old Dove asked mildly, "What is he shouting about? *At* someone?"

She had a fistful of white violets she had just gathered and was putting them into a small blue pitcher. She was a slight, thin child with a short-cut tumble of brown silk hair, intent gray eyes, a seashell mouth of a most delicate pink, and an air of lonely and intelligent independence.

Mrs. Nairn, her aunt, was having her midmorning coffee at the table by the window. She spooned in sugar. "Get yourself a glass of milk, Dove. I don't know who it is. I was upstairs doing his room and I saw a cab drive up, and she got out. The door was open and she walked right in, and was inside his workroom before I could get down the stairs to stop her."

Even three rooms away, and through the thick walls of the old house, his voice could be heard reverberating.

Drinking her milk, Dove asked, "It's not his woman, is it?"

Mrs. Nairn's mouth quirked at the corners but she said pointedly, "No, it's not his *friend* Mrs. Gaynor. I never saw her before but I must say she walked in as if she owned the place. Just like the lady of the house."

She finished her coffee. "Better get out into the sun again. You want to make the most of your holidays and I don't like you listening to some of those words he's saying."

Harley drew a long breath. He lowered the volume of his voice. "Have I made myself clear?"

"From your side of it, yes. It's my turn to make myself clear." Marta was sitting at one end of the sofa, in her crumpled creamy Irish tweed suit.

She was outwardly composed, but her heart gave one tremendous thump as she said, "You're very good at forgetting things you don't want on your mind. But you can't take a sponge to the slate and wipe away—three years ago on the seventeenth of March, at six o'clock, on Broken Saddle Road."

TWO

It was heavy, overcast, purple twilight, statistically a peak time for road accidents.

Harley had stayed longer than he intended to, drinking with his friend Mike Heard, the playwright. Must get home now, dine early, have a quiet sober evening before hitting the trail tomorrow, touting—his own expression—the new book on radio and television stations in New York, Philadelphia, Rochester, St. Louis, and Chicago. A week's breather, and then the Coast. It had all been set up by his publishers, Faunt and Faunt; he complained at great length about it and enjoyed it enormously.

A car coming toward him on Hunt's Lane reminded him by its headlights that he had forgotten in the thick dying day to turn his own on.

. . . Tomorrow, in Philadelphia, let's see, the dark gray vested suit. His maroon-and-white striped shirt, lighter gray knitted tie. If he said so himself he came over well on the television screen, the prominent bones, the big brilliant eyes. . . .

He turned right, into Broken Saddle Road. It dipped deep and swept high. Filthy Rich Road, he called it. Estates retreating, in immensities of money, far back from the macadam, pillared driveways, an occasional gatehouse.

Well, he wasn't far from filthy rich himself. And would be nearer if he could keep it up.

On his fortieth birthday, he had retired from the presidency of his large and profitable advertising agency. With money under his belt and time at his disposal, he had written his first novel, all six hundred pages of it. It had taken him just six months. It was entitled *The Wishing Wells* and was about the kings of petroleum in Arabia, New York, and Texas. It was also about money, power, sex, corruption, the United States Senate, more sex, and women.

(At Harley Ross, Inc., his biggest client had been Kyber Petroleum. When his book came out, Kyber's board talked about suing him and were only barely persuaded by their lawyers not to do so; it would only give substance, the lawyers said, to the man's mad meanderings.)

It wasn't just a big fat book; besides scandal, libel, and pornography, it had Harley's glee and lust and throbbing zest in it. Faunt and Faunt put a good deal of money into its launching and before publication it was bought by Janeway Films for $150,000.

"And where do you get your ideas for your books, Mr. Ross, or may I call you Harley?" Some idiot, interviewing him, often a woman, always attracted; he could feel the heat from them coming at him.

He was seeing himself from the camera's eye view, casually and wittily answering the idiot's question, when it happened.

He was taking a curve in the road. Something fast and white in the headlights—a big dog—flashed across in front of his car, making it safely to the other side. A child dashed after it. Harley's right fender hit the child and tossed it high in the air like an enormous doll. A split second later his left front wheel lifted thumpingly.

His mind and heart and breathing seemed to have stopped, but his ears recorded his own wild outcry and the screaming of the tires as he began to brake.

Then the car took over and refused to stop and turn back. The engine became a functioning mind, as his wasn't working. Flee, it told him, from horror, guilt, disaster, blood, and certainly death. Run, race away, the road's empty, no one behind, no one in front. Cocktail hour on Filthy Rich Road, everybody merrily drinking.

But, the car said, get off at the first right turning, there will be a car coming along Broken Saddle Road sooner or later, perhaps seconds from now. And keep the speed down, for God's sake. It swung its nose into Rawlinson Road, then chose another turn into Locker Street.

It wasn't your fault, it wasn't your *fault,* the engine purred at him. It couldn't have been avoided by the wildest miracle, the kid ran right under your wheels, totally invisible until then in the purple gloom. But hurry, hurry, get the hell home.

Marta was drinking a martini in front of the fire when the door crashed open and hit the wall and he stumbled over the doorstep and almost fell.

His voice was hoarse, and she saw that there were tears on his scarlet face. "Jesus Christ, I just killed a kid . . . Jesus, Jesus . . . it ran under the car and I panicked and ran, I should have stopped . . . Christ, with my hands shaking like this I can't . . . you get me the police and I'll tell them . . ."

His shoulders began to heave. The sound of his sobbing filled the room. Marta was standing very still, arms at her sides, breathing deeply to absorb and handle her shock.

"Are you crazy, Harley? And you about to start your book tour tomorrow?"

He stared at her as if he had never seen her before. "But that kid—there may be a chance, although God knows . . . Marta, for Christ's *sake* . . ."

"Fast, two things. Where? And were there other cars around?"

"No other cars that I could see . . . on a curve on the downside of that hill somewhere in the middle."

She closed her eyes, accurately summoned her mother's French-accented English, went to the telephone, and called the State Police barracks.

Sounding breathless and garbled was not difficult to manage. "Officer, there's been an accident, a child run over, on Broken Saddle Road . . . can you send the ambulance right away? . . . Yes, halfway down that big hill, there's a kind of pine forest on one side . . ."

She was handed over to another voice, wanting her to fill in details, and informing her that the ambulance was on the way.

She had, she said, been bicycling. In the headlights of a car coming toward her, perhaps eight feet away, she saw a dog and then a child running after it and she saw the car hit the child. "It could have been a girl or a boy, I don't know . . ."

She was going north and the car was heading south, toward Danbury. She had just moments ago passed a roadside telephone booth and not wanting to lose a second had turned back and placed her call.

Hard to tell in the dusk about the color of the car, some light color, and she had an impression of New York plates, "but you will comprehend, officer, under the circumstances I was hardly capable of observing *anything*. . . ."

Asked for her name and address, she crisply hung up.

Harley was shaking all over. His knees gave and he fell back onto the sofa. She went to the painted Dutch dresser, opened the lower doors, took out a bottle of brandy and poured him half a tumblerful.

"Thanks," he gasped, half choking on it, having to hold the glass with both hands. "For the call, I mean. For having a brain in your head . . ."

"This is only the beginning," Marta said. "The car. Let me think. It's bound to be marked. There may be blood. . . . Harley, finish your drink, go wash your face, tidy yourself up, I'll be back in a minute."

"Don't leave me *alone*," he begged. "I can't—"

"You must. And if anyone calls, let it ring a bit and say they got you out of the shower, that would explain your sounding all funny and out of breath."

She went to the kitchen for a flashlight and out the back door to the garage, where the car had decided it was better to hide itself. There was blood on the left front wheel, and a scrap of torn pink cloth caught in the grill. The right front fender was dented and there were spots where the paint had been ground off.

Her mind racing, she went back into the house. He was sitting where she had left him, his head hanging almost between his knees. He looked to be in a half faint.

He went over it aloud again, obsessively, the dog, the kid appearing from nowhere, the way the kid had seemed to hang in the air like a flying doll, his feeling of not being there at all but observing everything from a distance.

Marta said in a soothing, nursery voice, "Everything's done that can be done, as far as the child goes. It was obviously a hundred per cent not your fault, but there's no way of proving that, is there, there were no onlookers, no witnesses. That you know of. It's not the kind of night, it's below freezing, that people stroll about their estates."

Harley gave a hysterical caw of laughter, frightening to hear. "No witnesses except you, on your bicycle," he said.

"There'll be an alarm out for the car. But they think it's going south. I'll call you sometime tonight. . . ."

He thought he remembered seeing her go upstairs, come running down again in her coat, he couldn't name which coat it was, what color, and go out and close the kitchen door behind her.

But things were still terribly mixed up, he was still explaining out loud to the air around him. "Even if I'd stopped, what difference would it have made, nobody could have lived through . . . Have you any idea how much a car *weighs?*"

You shouldn't have left me alone, Marta. I'll go crazy.

He drained his drink and reached for the bottle.

Of course, she had to do something about the car. He whispered blurrily, "I'll never get into that car again."

From her mother, Marta had inherited Gallic common sense; from her German father, a stubborn see-it-through adherence to any project undertaken. From neither had she gotten the leavening of imagination, which in a way made her mission simpler.

The car must be disposed of. Well then, get on with it.

Harley had been going north when the accident happened—she deliberately turned off the word "death"—and the police informant reported it as going south.

If there was a lot of blood there would be, after the ambulance took the child away, blood on tire marks going in both directions. That didn't mean at all that she was safe from police scrutiny because she was going at first north and then northwest.

She drove through Still River, New Milford, and Kent, turned west, crossed into New York State and went north again. Wherever possible, she used back roads. She knew the way well. Her mother's summer house was in the little town of Amenia, in Dutchess County. She had the house keys in her pocket.

On leaving for several months in France, in early March, Berthe Burkhardt had said, "Whenever you can't stand that

man, which must be often—loudmouthed *brute,* egomaniac!—
you can retreat to my place.'' Harley and her mother's dislike
was mutual. Thriftily, Berthe had added, ''But don't charge
anything at my food market, I've closed my account until I
come back.''

The house stood in a grove of maples on a soaring hill half
a mile from the town center. It was white clapboard, modest
and pleasing outside, roomy and charmingly furnished within.
There was a great silence in the black night when she pulled
up in front of the garage and unlocked its doors. The nearest
house was perhaps an eighth of a mile away.

She put the car in the garage, went into the kitchen, brought
out a pailful of hot soapy water, and washed the left front and
rear tires, backing a few inches in the middle of the task to get
at the tire surfaces which had been resting on the cement floor.

Then she closed and padlocked the garage doors. The car
had almost a month's refuge, inside. Her mother's handyman,
who came once a week to clip the hedges and mow the lawn
and do odd chores for her, had no reason to enter it. His tools
and equipment were kept in another little stone building which
had once been a privy. He might, she thought, be useful later
on. Yes. Get him to paint the car pale yellow or perhaps green.
Then offer it to her greedy mother. ''Harley's buying me a
new one, I thought you might like to use this for errands and
save the wear and tear on the Mercedes.'' Mysterious impact
dents in the metal wouldn't trouble George Lasker; he was a
simple man, to whom everything had to be explained very
carefully. Her mother took advantage of this simplicity by
paying him wretchedly.

She went into the house, got herself a much-needed scotch,
and called Harley.

''It's all right. I'm at Mother's. I'd been planning to run up
here, remember, to see that George manured the borders and
started the topiary work on the hedges. I'll be back sometime
tomorrow.''

''All right? All *right?*'' His voice was thick and dazed. He
was drunk, as she had expected him to be, but she knew his
amazing powers of recovery.

''Take some aspirin and go to bed. Has anybody . . . called?''

''Nobody. Why would they?— A car heading south, a light-colored car with New York plates—'' and he was laughing that awful stomach-churning laugh again, veined through with tears.

"Harley, promise me. Take two aspirins and go to bed. It's almost eleven now, you have to be up at six. Good luck with your interview, call me after it. Everything is *absolutely* all right."

There was a long sigh, and then Harley said, "Everything is absolutely bloody hell, but thanks. . . ."

In the morning, she called a taxi to drive her to Newburgh, where she rented a car. It wouldn't do to arrive home in it; someone might wonder why, when the Rosses had two cars, one for each. Harley would have taken her blue Pontiac convertible this morning to drive to the little Mute airport where he had a chartered four-seater plane waiting to take him to Philadelphia. She left the rented car at the agency in New Milford, took another taxi to the airport, collected her Pontiac, and drove home.

The weekly Mute *Observer* was published the following day. It was front-page news:

SENATOR'S DAUGHTER VICTIM
OF FATAL HIT-AND-RUN TRAGEDY

Nine-year-old Lavinia Hyde, daughter of State Senator Ormond Hyde, was, according to medical authorities, killed instantly when she was struck by a car on Broken Saddle Road, where the 24-acre Hyde estate abuts. She had apparently been chasing her dog and state police say the dog probably returned to the child's body and was killed by another motorist in his vigil.

Marta felt a terrible chill taking her. My God, Hyde. It would be picked up by papers all through the state, maybe even get a mention in the New York *Times*. Hyde was rich, young, glamorous, just starting his plunge into politics.

The story went on to detail the telephone informant, the bicycling witness, a woman, with a slight French accent. A five-state alarm was out for the car. In their laboratory identification of paint chips deposited on the body, the police said that the car was a black 1976 Ford Nova. Garages in hundreds of towns and cities were being checked for a car that matched this description, brought in for repair or retouching.

Thank God, Marta thought, that Harley spurned the notion of a car adding anything to a man's status, and always bought and drove the cheapest, most anonymous and nearly invisible models available—the Nova being more or less anonymous to anyone but, say, a boy buying his first car, or the design department of the Ford Motor Company.

She smiled without mirth when she came to a police theory that the so-called bicyclist might very probably be the culprit, overtaken by guilt, stopping at the Broken Saddle Road phone booth not far from the scene of the accident and calling upon them to send an ambulance.

Running in the next column was a story about "our local eminent man of letters, Harley Ross," who was to appear this afternoon on Station WLDB in Philadelphia to discuss his new book, *Kingdom Come*. The paper regretted that the Philadelphia station could not be picked up in Mute but informed its readers that they could look forward to his appearance on the "Today Show" in New York on Friday.

It was unofficially considered by the police a pretty hopeless hunt, unless there was some wild unlikely lucky break.

Broken Saddle Road, although closed to buses and trucks, was a link between highways to those who knew the countryside. You went south and west on it if you wanted Danbury, Long Island Sound, Greenwich, New York. North and east if you were heading for Hartford or New Haven.

The town of Mute itself had a population of fifty-five hundred. Car registrations were gone through. Seven hundred people in the town and surrounding villages, owners of black Fords, were interviewed.

Marta, although she didn't know it, was home free before the first question was put to her.

Young Sergeant Pelone, wearily pursuing his thirty-fifth check—goddamn wild-goose chase—was impressed and a little embarrassed in his approach to the Ross residence.

A long pleasant gray stone house, old, restored, set well back from the road in ten acres of woods and meadows. French windows opening on a semicircle of lawn, snowy now and slick with a crust of ice. A steep sheer rock face rising as a natural shelter behind the house, with an icicle-bearded slender waterfall coming down from its high lip into a birch-rimmed pool.

One car in the garage. Blue.

He had called Marta early and said he wanted a few words with her, a routine car check. Shaking inside, she put together a well-calculated blend of sexiness and domesticity.

The woman who opened the door to him wore a workmanlike blue canvas apron over long-legged gray flannel pants and a creamy open-throated shirt. The color of the apron, he noticed, exactly matched her eyes. The winter sun struck her buttery shining hair, with its thick braided chignon. A smell of bread baking floated in the air, the very scent of homely peace and virtue.

He removed his gaze from the handsome lift of the breasts under the apron bib. Strong sort of woman, he thought, but soft . . . nice and soft, she would be.

Yes, they did indeed own a black Ford. No, she didn't know the name of the model, she never noticed car's nicknames. Her mother had borrowed it— "Let's see," Marta said, going to a lacquered green desk by a window and studying a little gold-framed calendar—"I know it was a Saturday. Yes, the tenth of March."

Don't, *don't* fill in too many details. "Transmission troubles with hers. She lives in Amenia, New York, and—"

"That's okay, then."

Don't, in your relief, offer him a cup of coffee, don't in any way say thank you, officer.

Turning to go, he said, "I saw your husband, Harley—Mr. Ross on the "Today Show" yesterday, he was great, he can be a very funny guy, can't he? Me, I wouldn't have the nerve to get in front of all those cameras, I'd clam up for sure. Thanks, Mrs. Ross, have a good day, now."

THREE

"Let's look at this, not as a war but as a practical civilized arrangement," Marta said. "It will be so much easier that way."

Harley was at his desk, head in his hands. He took his hands away and looked not at her but across the room. From dangerously royal-red colorings his face had turned damp and pale. Even his wide mouth, with its deep, lifted, elfin corners, had gone a sort of blue.

God, she thought, is he going to have some kind of attack, psychosomatic or otherwise, or both?

He got up from his chair, went over to the fireplace, and in a tired used-up way gave a half savage kick at a log, which hurt his toes badly through his handmade English leather shoe.

"Let's not look at this as blackmail, in other words," he said, addressing the mantelpiece. "And thinking back, you did what you did as much for yourself as for me, or more so. Your London Bridge was falling down. . . ."

He was only vaguely aware of what he was saying.

After the first stunned verbal vomiting of outrage, of refusal to look at and accept and live with, even for a short time, the impossible, he was suddenly numb. Except for the toes of his right foot, which were still suffering from the presence of this invading bitch.

"As far as the great world goes," Marta said, trying to sound serene for both of them, it wouldn't do to have him buckle under a heart attack, "the less said the better. We're back together. People do it all the time. Look at the Gordons."

17

She went and leaned against the windowsill with the apple trees and dandelioned meadow at her back. Against the sunny April afternoon, she was a dark, strong, looming shape.

"And as to immediate matters . . . I won't interrupt your way of life at all. Your working time will be sacrosanct, of course. I'll take the pink room across the hall from . . ."

In a vague, convalescent's voice, he said, "You're not to do anything about Mrs. Nairn, anything at all."

"Who is Mrs. Nairn?"

"My housekeeper."

"She seems to do an excellent job, the place is shining. Who's that child I saw with violets she'd just picked?"

"Dorothea Something . . . Mrs. Nairn's niece, the woman has the care of her for some reason . . . called Dove I think. . . ." He yawned tremendously and closed his eyes. If her voice stopped, he thought he might sleep. He couldn't remember when he had been this tired.

"Of course I won't do anything about her, I told you it's going to be a civilized arrangement, the house run for your comfort. As well as mine. And we'll both behave better, more naturally, won't we, with eyes and ears around. Sometimes it's a good thing to be onstage. Cools the temper and calms the voice."

He opened his eyes and yawned again. "What the hell are you talking about?"

"Gone off again, Harley, escaping, the way you do?" Kindly, "You've had enough adjusting for the moment. Suppose we practice reunited husband and wife in front of Mrs. Nairn." She glanced at her watch. "Close to lunchtime. Let's have a drink and—I don't want to put her off this first day—suppose you tell her what to do about lunch. Something substantial, I was up at five o'clock this morning."

Marching orders. Even though her voice was soft and amiable. Fantastic.

"I work until two in case you've forgotten. Go get your own food and drink from her." He heard with alarm the small-boy sulkiness in his voice. When he recovered himself, he'd get his rage back, and his strength. This could and would and had to be dealt with. But not right now.

He wanted badly to put his face back into his hands and weep.

"As you please," Marta said, and went out and closed the door behind her.

He sat and stared at the typewriter. He had had the next scene all but blocked out in his head and now it had vanished; there was just a gray humming where the working mind should be. A lost two hours or so this morning wouldn't be fatal, he had already done seven pages, twenty-one hundred words, since seven-thirty. But tomorrow, and the next day—would he be able to work at *all?*

The typewriter put him in mind of a slain creature, forever silenced.

He suddenly thought, does she mean she's here for *life?* For all her life, for all my life?

Or was her plan temporary food, shelter, clothing, funds, until another Mandarino turned up.

They had both met Mandarino at a party in New York. He was introduced to them as "the portrait painter, you know. And has a divine gallery." Harley said to Marta, "I'll bet that dago sleeps with all his subjects." On the way to their room at the St. Regis five hours later, Marta said, "He wants to paint me." Harley, openhanded in most things, had certain thrifts he hewed to. He was not only not interested in art, in pictures, he was capable of looking at them without seeing them at all.

"If you have enough in your own balance to pay him, go ahead. But don't say I didn't warn you."

She went ahead. He was aware that there was something on the boil-and-bubble between the two; but he was plunging joyfully through the last quarter of his book and he looked the other way.

At that time he still thought of her as his home base, his rock. Hell, let them go on with it and get it over, perhaps she deserved a short spin. Maritally speaking, she wasn't the wanderer he was.

Two weeks after her portrait was finished—"My God, he's made you look like an earth mother stranded on the Russian steppes," Harley said, shouting with laughter—and six weeks from the time of the first meeting, she left her husband.

*   *   *

Marta walked with straight-backed confidence into the kitchen. It was immaculate and empty. A delicious smell of tomatoes and bay drifted from a covered pot on the stove. Through one of the big windows she saw a woman who must be Mrs. Nairn down on her hands and knees in front of what was evidently going to be a flower border at the foot of the birches rimming the pool; the earth was freshly spaded up. She was handing seeds from a sweet pea packet to the child—Birdie, wasn't it?—and the small forefinger poked each seed to knuckle depth.

Going out the door, Marta raised her voice a little to be heard above the waterfall. "Hello. You're Mrs. Nairn?"

Mrs. Narin got to her feet. She was a small thin woman of a tough sturdy build. She had a keenly boned plain face, short graying red hair, and perceptive fair-lashed gray eyes. She looked alert, efficient, and very much her own woman, in her plaid jersey shirt and pants.

"I'm Mrs. Ross."

"Mrs. . . . Who, Ross?" There was nothing rude or impudent about it; the other woman simply wanted information.

"Mrs. Harley Ross. Railway Express will be bringing around my bags and things later on this afternoon. If I'm not here will you see to them? I'll be in the pink room. Is there anything, by the way, to eat? I'm starving."

"Yes, there is," Mrs. Nairn said briskly, no trace of servility about her. "Mr. Ross occasionally likes soup for his lunch, today it's tomato bouillon. Or, if you'd rather, a cheese omelet and a salad."

"That sounds lovely. And just a cup of the soup to start with."

"Mrs. *Harley* Ross?" Dove took a while to ask it; she liked to absorb, ponder, and mentally explore matters before seeking extra facts. "His?" She dipped a hungry spoon into Mrs. Nairn's soup, into which she had crumbled soda crackers.

Mrs. Nairn was always direct with her; she was a remarkably intelligent child and from time to time they spoke to each other as equals. Her sister, Ellie, had been killed in an automobile

accident when Dove was three. Tom Harlan, her father, was
a salesman of electronic equipment and traveled from coast to
coast all year long, stopping by five or six times during the
year, with hugs and warmth and love and terrible goodbyes to
Dove. But Mrs. Nairn, Aunt Em, was essentially her mother
and her world.

At the sink, washing Marta's luncheon dishes, she said,
"She left him a couple of years ago, as far as I know, went
off with someone else. And now as far as I can gather she's
back. We don't know for how long, we haven't heard a word
from him."

"Except for all that roaring. This morning. *Bitch* . . ." She
said the word experimentally, with grave interest.

"Mind your tongue, Dove. It's after two, I haven't heard a
word out of him, I'd better—"

She went to the door of his workroom and knocked. After
a moment the door was opened and she looked, shocked, at
Harley, standing there with the knob in his hand. He's like a
great joyous floating pink balloon, she thought, that's been
pierced and deflated by a pin. Drink, was it? No . . . but his
eyes were vague and he seemed to be looking at her without
recognition.

"You're past your time for lunch, Mr. Ross, I thought I'd
take my courage into my hands and see to your stomach."
Strange, uncomfortable feeling; she had been in charge of his
house for two years, in charge of his working privacy, and his
meals, and his stomach. Now, she had no idea whether she'd
be responsible for managing these things any longer; or if so,
under someone else's superior orders.

When her husband had died, the same year as her sister,
Ellie, she had had two choices. Brush up on her shorthand and
typing and take some ghastly grinding clerical job in Hartford
or New Haven; or go into domestic service, and keep Dove at
her side, no lonely child half-looked after by bored baby sitters.
She enjoyed cooking and didn't mind cleaning. And there was
a certain relish in spending money not her own to run a comfortable, pleasant house.

(At school, girls said to Dove, "Your aunt's a housekeeper?
A *servant?*" Dove had anxiously brought the inquiries home

and Mrs. Nairn said, "Your pride's in your bones, not in the
label that they hang on what you do for an honest living.")

There were things about Harley Ross she didn't approve of,
but it had been a happy sort of time, working for him, Dove
with her own little back bedroom looking straight into the
waterfall, she with her big room and bath next to it, good
money, peace and quiet and a security that had seemed without
end.

To break his silence, which was worrying her, she said,
"I've given Mrs. Ross her lunch, I think she's gone upstairs
for a nap."

The ordinarily big, rich voice, now deflated too, didn't sound
like him at all. "Mrs. Ross . . . oh, yes. She's just passing
through, she won't be here long, Mrs. Nairn. We'll just put
up with her. For the time being."

He mixed and drank his two martinis, told her he didn't want
his soup, thank you, and instead of going up to his bed for his
nap went back into the workroom and closed the door. She
heard the snap of the bolt on the inside, shot home.

As if, she thought, he was barricading himself. Against *her*.

The interval after lunch was the same as every day. Almost.

Mrs. Nairn, his—*their?*—house in shining order, after her
morning's work, went up to her bedroom. She poured a small
scotch from a bottle scrupulously provided by herself for herself, settled in a soft deep chair by the window and began
reading, for the fourth time since the age of twenty-five, Jane
Austen's *Mansfield Park*.

A woman who heard and felt not only through her ears but
through her nerves and intuition, she recorded that Mrs. Harley
Ross was solidly entrenched. And probably asleep, victorious,
in the room across the hall from Harley's.

And that the silent house was thrumming with rage.

Dove, searching for Custard, her young pale yellow cat,
found her in the greening honeysuckle under the windows of
Mr. Ross's workroom. For some reason that she didn't under-
stand, troubled and wanting company, she draped Custard over
her forearm.

Across the room, not near the window, his voice said, "I won't have it, Christ Almighty . . . I won't have it—" And then there was a sound that if Mr. Ross wasn't grown up might be thought of as a gasping sob.

The sort of noise she made when she was running, and fell, and badly scraped a knee. Shock and fury and pain.

She took Custard into the apple orchard, and lay on her back on the cool long grass, and soothed and lost herself in watching the immense white clouds floating steadily east, overhead. One was an elephant, one a leaping deer, and one, round, with blue holes in it, was Mr. Ross's large-eyed hairless head.

And then another huge one, menacing, with a great swollen gray underneath, looking as if it could fall on you and blot you out. Not wanting to cope with her fleeting feeling of woe, of the end of contentment, Dove turned on her side in the sweet soft grass and fell asleep.

What heaven, what absolute heaven, Marta thought, drowsing between her cornflower-printed white linen Porthault sheets. Nice room, she'd never slept in it before, great comfortable canopied bed.

Sooner or later, after he got over his spasms, Harley might want her back in with him. He probably couldn't hold out indefinitely against the temptation of the known, naked body across the hall.

But don't push it. She heard a clattering below the front windows. Good, her bags arriving. It would have been interesting to observe Harley's face when he saw this indication of permanent residence.

Some chemistry was working within Harley. He had been down as deep as he could go. Now there was no direction open to him but up.

Standing by the window, he composed a sentence in his head: "He was like a great beast, lying low, contained and waiting, calculating the exact instant when he would leap, blood, kill, extinguish his prey."

He remembered a technique from his advertising days, useful with associates, employees, and clients. Put people off their balance by behaving *as they did not expect you to behave*. This confused and unmanned them, made their own footing slippery.

He went upstairs, glared at Marta's closed door, drew himself a hot bath and lay soaping and soaking in it for fifteen minutes. He dressed in flannels and a pale lilac pongee shirt, one of a dozen he had had made for himself in Hong Kong.

When, freshly showered herself, Marta came downstairs at five-thirty she found him reading the New York *Times* in the living room. His comfort well in hand, a fire of fragrant apple logs blazing, a martini on the table beside him which he was sipping in a leisurely way, a bowl of mixed nuts, a plate of crackers and Caerphilly cheese.

"I give," he would say on occasion, "a very decent cocktail party for myself when people are obliging enough to leave me alone."

He lifted his eyes from his paper and gazed at her as she stopped, for just a second or so hesitating, in the broad doorway. She had changed from her suit into a long soft red wool Galanos and as usual in the house was barefooted.

"Still a peasant from the ankles down," he said with his great merry white-toothed grin. "That dress held up well. But then it ought to, as I recall it cost me twelve hundred dollars."

Was he drunk? No. The rich voice had clear vibrating edges. "And do you still drink martinis?"

"Still do."

"When you can afford them, that is. Well, I happen to have the makings for an entire vat of martinis." He went to the painted dresser and mixed her drink. He handed it to her with bland politeness.

Not wanting to share the sofa with this dangerously good-tempered sociable man, she chose the wing chair on the other side of the hearth.

"Cheers." He lifted his half-full glass to her. "Now. Practical matters. I heard an awful commotion, I suppose your luggage being delivered. What's your financial position?"

"Zero," Marta said. "And I owe a lot of bills and things."

"You certainly got here in the nick of time," Harley observed with another immense grin. "Didn't you?"

She left this unanswered and he went on, "No necessity to

open an account for you, feel free to use my checkbook.''

"Why? Why no separate account, I mean?"

"It's easier for my tax man. Demanding fellow, you'd wonder who's working for whom. He makes me use American Express for any and all business expenses so his life will be easier. . . ."

"But you'll be gnashing your teeth when you see the stubs I've filled in," Marta said, frowning. "It's a sort of invasion of privacy. Mine."

He threw back his head and roared with laughter. The sound filled the room and bounced off the walls. *"An invasion of privacy.* I'd forgotten your refreshing lack of any sense of humor whatever. But then it came in handy at parties. No competition from my mate in that line.''

The telephone on the table at the other end of the sofa rang. Harley put up a deterring hand. "Mrs. Nairn always answers it when she's here, on her own extension. Keeps egregious nuisances off my back. Bear it in mind and don't grab—"

From the doorway, Mrs. Nairn said, "Mrs. Hyde, Mr. Ross."

A flare of blood suffused Harley's face.

I'm back on top, Marta thought jubilantly. Right back up on top.

Harley's voice was under perfect control. Holding the receiver, he said, "Why *not!*" after a few seconds of listening. "Nine o'clock? Yes . . . and I'll have a surprise up my sleeve for you, Alison.''

He hung up and turned to Marta. "They have a congressman who wants to meet the great Harley Ross. I didn't know congressmen could read. Would you like to accompany me, after your no doubt exhausting trek here from wherever you've been holed up?''

"Yes, I would," Marta said. "The sooner everybody knows, the sooner it will blow over and settle down.''

"Have you worked out a cover story for our supposedly fond reunion? Or are you leaving that to me, as a writer of fiction?''

"Just that we wanted to be together again. As I said this morning, look at the Gordons.''

"You're not up to date on the Gordons. Their second go-round didn't last. He ran amok one night while he was carving a leg of lamb and chased her all over the house with the knife. Fortunately, she escaped in one piece. I suppose he'd had a drink or so but still—which reminds me.'' He got up and made himself another martini.

A ravishing scent of shallots in wine and simmering butter floated into the room. ''Practical matters again—'' Harley took a thirsty gulp of his drink. ''Mrs. Nairn has through trial and error found out what I like and cooks it marvelously. Don't put yourself to any lady-of-the-manor trouble, dictating menus to her. Leave it in her hands. And she shops like a French-woman, haggles and scolds and tyrannizes if everything isn't just right.''

Marta opened her mouth and closed it again.

This was her house, not Mrs. Nairn's.

But there would be plenty of time for Harley to learn to adapt.

FOUR

"Brief me," Marta said, "on the Hydes and you. We hadn't met them before my departure."

"She was at a party at Joe Grundy's, you don't know him, he's a sculptor, newish here. She liked me, simple as that. They invite me to things. Fame and fortune are no hindrance to popularity. Nor being unattached, of course." A muscle twitched in his cheek like a deep sudden dimple. "Just to fill you in, they have two surviving children."

Harley had maintained his hard blitheness all through dinner and still wore it, aggressively and protectively, as they turned in from Broken Saddle Road to the Hydes' driveway.

For the first time since she had come back, Marta offered placating words to the man beside her. "Drink whatever you want, I'll drive us home. Turn and turn about, remember? Although it was my turn to be good more often than it was yours."

"I'd forgotten you so completely—amazing, isn't it?—that I'll have to bone up on us. In case anyone asks. Yes, now I do remember. One on tomato juice or ginger ale and the other having a hell of a time."

"It is amazing, after eight years," Marta said, "but as I pointed out you're good at wiping the slate."

He had met her nine years ago at a dinner party given by one of his clients, Thomas Cady, of the Cady Mutual Fund; she was then Marta Cady. He was at once struck by her blue and gold, rosy stillness and solidity. "By God," he said to himself, "there's a *woman*. She's like some kind of monument

27

to herself.'' Over wine and dinner, he calculated the exact measurements of her breasts and thighs while he told funny stories about a day in the life of an advertising man. He wondered if her serene silence meant depths under shining still waters or mere stupidity and thought it didn't matter one way or another.

His wife, Adele, now divorced from him, had been a tremendous talker, and some people thought she was funnier and more interesting and talented than he was.

He lost the Cady account but gained Marta. ''You have no idea how dull it is to live with mutual funds,'' she said. ''And you're going to be a *writer*.'' She gave the word a holy sound, a priestliness.

They had had five or six nice years until Harley's affairs increased in pace with his own self-celebration and his mild boredom with her; and they drifted into living like the outwardly married but the inwardly separate and alone.

Ormond Hyde opened the door of the long terraced white house to them. He was a tall fair man who looked like an attractive parrot, beaked nose, bright eyes, forehead and chin in long opposing slopes.

''Harley! And . . . ?''

''We'll let you know inside,'' Harley said. He had changed after dinner into a superb ruddy Harris tweed suit; he liked making entrances, and even this bizarre one gave him a curious thump of satisfaction. At least four of the dozen or so people in the living room would know who the woman at his side was.

With a hard elfin grin, he bent his head and whispered. ''Over to you.''

There was a sudden wave of silence cutting into the party thrum of voices. Then, ''Marta! Well, I'll be damned!'' shouted a man's voice from across the room, and Bob Ingram came over and gave her a hearty hug. ''What's all this?''

In a voice not loud but clear and lifted, she said, ''We've joined forces again. Wasn't it helpful that Harley was too lazy to divorce me? Saves us the trouble of getting married all over.''

Introductions were made. To Alison Hyde, slender, pale, and ashen-haired, Marta said, ''I do hope you don't mind your

uninvited mystery guest? It's a nice way to celebrate. It's—us,
I mean—just happened."

Alison Hyde, who felt an honest deep bewilderment, found
it hard to rally immediately and say the bright, worldly, expected things. It wouldn't do at all to start with, I've heard so
much about you.

"Our mystery guest is welcome, lovely to meet you. Both
of you come and meet the congressman. Knowing you, Harley,
you can cut him off at the source, he's been going on and on
about the Ways and Means Committee." God, why couldn't
she stop talking?

(Later, when they were undressing, she said to Ormond,
"But what about Jill? I thought that they were up to here in
it? Lucky she's in Paris. Lucky for *somebody*.")

("Way of the world, darling. People taking in each other's
washing. She has something, you must admit.")

("She seems to have Harley," Alsion said.)

Harley was in top form, center stage, surrounded by people,
a bonfire throwing off light and crackling vitality. He flirted,
he made other people feel uproariously amusing, and all the
time he was running what Alison called the Harley Ross Revue.
Telling stories, interrupted in the middle of them by his own
anticipatory, gasping, infectious laughter. She thought he
sounded a little manic tonight, hysterical, but she had heard
him that way on other occasions, drunk with the excitement of
being himself, Harley.

Marta sat on a sofa with Bob Ingram, the two of them deep
in a murmur of reminiscences; Ingram had thought himself a
little in love with her before her Mandarino turned up.

One guest, seeing her drinking her tomato juice and switching
later to iced coffee, asked, "Is she A.A.?"

"I don't think so . . . or certainly wasn't before she left
him. For a freshly reunited wife, she seems awfully content
with another man, doesn't she?"

"You know Harley, when he gets started he doesn't need
anybody but himself."

Representative Milne said peevishly to Alison, "Fellow's

like a Roman emperor, isn't he? Strides in and takes over.''
He had had considerably more information he wished to air on
the current activities of the House Ways and Means Committee.

''Well, if writers weren't inclined to be articulate, where
would we all be?'' Alison started to move away and, not wanting
to lose this ashy beauty and be left alone, another listener on
the outer edge of Harley's circle, Milne grasped her forearm
and nodded his head at the silver-framed photograph of a small
girl who looked very much like his hostess, face-on in the
bookshelves between mellow bindings.

''Which little kiddy is that, I suppose she's in bed?''

''No,'' Alison said. ''She's dead. I'm so sorry, but I must
see to some empty glasses.''

At intervals during the night, he found himself sweating in
vivid waking nightmares.

Slightly misquoting Edna St. Vincent Millay, he thought—or
had he said it aloud?—''I was so gay, I was so merry, I rode
back and forth all night on the ferry.''

While all the time . . .

At any minute she could have opened her full-lipped mouth
and said, ''Look, Alison, look, Ormond, there he is, he's the
one who . . .''

He had told her more or less correctly that he had forgotten
her completely. And two years had passed, had maybe done
deep-down things to her. What did he know about her mental
balance?

What did he know about the reasons for her return? The
obvious ones were the easiest to live with, however hideously
unwelcome the presence: a desire for financial security, a roof
over her head, an ordered stable existence.

But what if vengeance against the things that had happened
to her, or a heady sense of absolute power, took over?

She could have destroyed him, at the Hydes', in five or six
words.

Christ, what if she went into early menopause and went off
her nut as some women seemed to do?

She was, let's see, forty-two. With her robust health, she
could well live until at least eighty; that miserly bitch of a

mother, at sixty-five, still looked to be in her skinny prime. I'll give *myself* another twenty-five years at the most, Harley thought, at the awful black-winged hour of four in the morning.

She'll outlive me, she'll live on and on, here in this house, on my money, with my name fastened to her, reclaimed by her. Mrs. Harley Ross, widow of the prolific best-selling novelist . . .

Unless it was a game, a scheme, a plan, something that would only take a week, a month, before she moved on to other fields.

He turned on his side and crashed a fist into the other pillow on the double bed, the place where her head used to lie. But all my *life*, he thought in soaking terror. If it's really as simple as it looks, her return, it means every second, every minute, every hour and day of the rest of my life.

And even then—accepting the reasonable surface explanation—if he wasn't *nice* to her always, if there was any everyday kind of trouble, any quarrel, any flare of temper on her part, any sudden desire for drama, she could decide to . . .

He found himself shaking with sobs and snatched himself back from a brink. Normal, he assured himself. Putting on that act with her last night, and then taking over at the party, going off like a Fourth of July sparkler touched with a lighted match. Soar up that high, you have to expect a corresponding plunge.

And of course this is the worst hour of the night. Sick people sink and die at this hour. Well and happy people, waking at four, stumble on terrors they never knew lay at the back of their heads.

And because he found his visions unbearable, some safety valve flicked on and sent him into bottomless sleep.

He woke as usual at seven and lay for a moment refreshed and buoyant. And then full awareness hit him like a hammer swung against his skull.

Marta.

I'll cope one way or another, he told himself with fierce briskness. Look at all the appalling business problems I've solved for clients. There's a way out of everything if you put your mind and your skills to it.''

FIVE

He took a long hot encouraging shower, dressed, and found himself tiptoeing down the stairs as if to keep a sleeping baby from waking. She hadn't used to get up early, but what if she'd changed her ways?

The clean peaceful kitchen was no longer his. Making coffee, drinking his orange juice, he listened intently and jumped when the morning wind blew an apple tree branch against the near window.

Today would be his first full day as a married man, again.

Well, at least it wouldn't get in the way of his work. At the typewriter, he could brush her aside, out of existence.

Yes, it would.

No, it wouldn't.

He'd been able to work when he was coming down with pneumonia; there had been only a half-hour interlude between ending a chapter and climbing into a hospital bed.

He'd been able to work after reading, with his orange juice, the worst review of his life, in the New York *Times*. It began: "Credit where credit is due. Harley Ross is the hands-down master of classy trash, which he delivers by the pound in *A Thunder of Eagles*."

And the morning after Marta left him, he had done as he well remembered eleven pages.

He found himself staring tensely at the open door into the kitchen, waiting for the figure to appear in it, almost soundless on her bare feet. Even though she wasn't there she *was* there, rosily nourished by sleep, hair shiningly braided and chignoned.

"It's not fair that the whites of your eyes are so goddamned white in the morning," he used to say to her. "Look at mine!"

Still tiptoeing, his large tall body in an unaccustomed stooping scurry, he made for the haven of his workroom; spilling coffee, in his speed, on the bird-patterned Tabriz living-room rug.

Now.

Now everything was going to be all right. He flipped the cover off his electric typewriter, which he cared for as lovingly as a trainer would a valuable horse. He had a personal passion for the beautiful, obedient, inspired machine. He flicked the switch and beamed at the soft ticking purr as the typewriter started living, breathing, ready for work.

He lit his first cigarette and gulped his first mouthful of coffee, wheeled in a fresh sheet of yellow paper, and sat with his hands hovering over the keys.

Christ, what was wrong with his hands, his fingers? They felt stiff, sculpted here in air, like stone, like marble. He rubbed and kneaded them together, hard. He picked up and read the last of the pages he had written yesterday.

Before the knock, before "Go away," before Marta.

He had been just going into the kind of scene that should have written itself. Well, get a sentence down anyway, unfreeze his hands, make marks on paper.

"Knowing it was a life and death matter, death of the heart—" Hell, no, that was a title of Elizabeth Bowen's, but change it later, "she opened the bedroom door and"—and what? Were the other two awake? Asleep? Making love?

A portion of one sentence, he discovered, had taken an entire cigarette and a whole cup of coffee. He got up to make fresh coffee on the electric plate. Normally he didn't get around to this until he'd been working for forty-five minutes.

Okay, play it full strength, they're making love when she opens the door, what does she do, what does she say?

"No. She's dead. I'm so sorry but I must see to . . ."

He had been standing four feet away from creamy silvery Alison when she answered Representative Milne's question about the child in the silver frame, in the bookcase.

From nowhere a burning question entered his mind.

What had she finally done, about the car?

It had been stashed in her mother's garage, in Amenia; the old twister was safely in France for six weeks or so. "Don't worry, I'll think of something. Just get on with your tour. You were awfully good in San Francisco last night, and I'm sure nobody but me knew that you'd had just one too many. Too many for anybody else, that is, but for you it works wonders."

Several weeks after he had gotten back from his last stop, Seattle, he had asked reluctantly, hesitantly—he was already visibly steaming with a new plot he was excited about—"Marta, the car?"

"Thoroughly taken care of, disposed of, no problem forever more, but I won't tell you, you might absentmindedly put it into a book or have a guilty extra drink with a close friend and— You know what I mean."

"Oh," Harley said, out loud, on this new and ruined April morning, *"God."*

She knew where it was, the car; he didn't. It could be fetched out, examined. His fatal dossier in injured metal. He could deny that he had rushed home and told her his terrible story. But the car was her proof, her ace.

He had in two years almost managed to veil it, thrust it away, scrub his mind of it, the grief and guilt and shock. When it occasionally came back to scald him, he heard the voice saying, "It was obviously one hundred per cent not your fault." and agreed, but the voice hadn't been in the car and hadn't felt the thump of the wheel over flesh and bone and life.

She had brought it all back with her, in her Gucci luggage. Unpacked it and set it out, fresh and immediate, before his shrinking senses.

He got up and paced his workroom, that lovely safe place where he was always so absorbed, so happy. A wall of books, a stone fireplace, a pleasantly shabby Chinese rug, a two-story ceiling of liberating height, six windows, three of them looking out on the waterfall and occasionally splattered by it when the wind was high. Diamond lights pouring down the walls, racing over the rug and the chestnut-stained hardwood rim of floor around it. Usually the reflections stimulated him, reminded him of his own brain, functioning in this special place like colored lightning.

Enraged by the mocking flickers—we're still in business, why aren't you?—he pulled the never-used shades to the sills and went over and lay down on his leather sofa. But the falling water sounds remained, to scourge him. Rush, splash, pour, in joyous crystal energy.

After a few minutes the drawn shades reminded him of a house of mourning and he snapped them back up again.

A house of mourning. Dear departed Harley Ross, although he looks alive, doesn't he? No, it's his typewriter that died. Cover it decently. He hadn't realized until now what a blissfully happy man he had been until close to noon yesterday, when everything stopped.

A house of mourning. Too bad, she was only forty-two. . . . Yes, very sudden. Of—*what?*

He made a startled choked sound in his throat and did something that he normally disallowed while working.

Working?

He got a bottle of scotch out of his desk drawer and poured a third of a tumblerful.

Have you heard about poor bumbling Ross? Down the drain. Some chapters just don't make any sense at all.

This was intolerable. A man could think himself to death, to suicide, or some other kind of destruction. Move. Function. *Do something.*

He seized upon an idea that had come to him in the night, just after his vision of Marta with a terribly sharp shiny knife in her hand, the knife pointed straight at his heart and not two inches away from the breathless flesh.

She was sitting at what had been her end of the sofa, drinking coffee, deep in his *Times*. She looked just as he had imagined her in the kitchen doorway, rested and pink. She wore a long white terry robe and he could smell the soap she always used, sandalwood.

She looked as though she had never been away.

"Good morning, Harley. I thought it took a hurricane or a

fire to flush you out of your workroom before two. Have you changed your ways?''

He stood with his hands in his pockets, looking down at her. "No. An emergency's come up, remember? I thought I'd deal with it first and then resume my labors."

Careful. Don't get her mad.

"I did a lot of thinking last night, Marta—naturally. It's madness for two people who no longer have any emotional bond—two strangers—to chain themselves to each other."

"Spoken like a writer," Marta said, smiling. "That isn't the way I see it at all, but go on."

"I'm prepared to offer you a certain amount of money on a regular basis. We'd work out the sum." He kept his face calm, but he could feel the color of rage beginning under the skin of his face and neck. Blackmailing bitch. "You're here presumably because you're broke. I know you were never brought up to turn your hand to anything, so okay, following a brief friendly meeting after two years, Harley and Marta decide on a permanent separation and he agrees to undertake her support."

"And how much did you have in mind?"

"Maybe—I don't know—twenty thousand." The sound of it, the burden of it, appalled him, and before he could stop himself he added, "As long as I was good for it—"

"It would take twice that, perhaps three times that, to live the way I live here," Marta said, as calmly as if she were discussing the price of coffee. "You know that, Harley. Besides—I'd thought it over too—it wouldn't look good. People, knowing your ways with money, might think you were paying me a kind of blood money. They might start thinking, wondering, going back to before I left, nosing around— But in any case, you *might* be able to afford proper upkeep in your good years, but you wouldn't. This is far more practical. And a lot cheaper for you."

Her manner as much as her words said a flat and final no.

He felt his hands balling into fists in his pockets. He wanted to snatch her off the sofa, strike her, send her crashing against the wall, watch her fall broken to the floor, and turn and leave her there.

"Well, don't say I didn't try to avoid the worst, for both of us," he said. He had no idea where the thought, the words had come from: They just exploded into the air.

Going up the stairs to do his bedroom and bathroom, Mrs. Nairn heard the cold savagery of his voice, the violence just barely contained, and felt something like a shiver pass over her.

I wonder, she thought, if this is a good place for Dove to be in, a safe place. The air of the house had subtly altered since Mrs. Ross's return, and suggested the held-breath stillness that precedes a cataclysmic storm.

But, nonsense. She shouldn't drink such strong tea in the morning, two cups to it, she always felt a little odd an hour later.

Just Harley, a man of explosions. Look at the noises he made all by himself, in the workroom.

She ought to be used to it by now.

Tomorrow morning, a cup of Dove's cocoa, and skip the tea.

S I X

While not the musical-comedy stage set for major and minor names and talents that Westport had become, Mute and its environs had a cluster of luminaries, writers, artists, the sculptor Joe Grundy, a symphony conductor and a satellite of composers and musicians, and others that Harley described as "of like ilk." After his five years in Mute and Marta's three, a good many of them were friends or at least party companions.

On the morning after Marta Ross returned to her husband, dials were spun, receivers lifted.

"Ain't love grand? Marta's back with Harley, after lighting off with that Greek."

"Italian. Ann Tree said she was broke, had gone through any number of men, and was working somewhere, sales-clerking, I forget—oh, Helena Rubinstein. Ann ought to know. She's an old friend of Marta's."

"But how *kind* of Harley to take her back. It doesn't sound like him at all."

The woman who was living with Joe Grundy said, into her telephone, "I don't get it. What about Jill? I've never met the Ross woman, she must be brave, I'd sooner take a fresh kill from a Bengal tiger with my bare hands. . . ."

From his studio, Grundy shouted, "You've done it any number of times!"

"We were right there, last night, at the Hydes' with the two of them," Polly Ingram reported to a friend. "Harley was fantastic, doing his stuff. She looked awfully good in that way she has, someone wandering out of the wings in a Wagner

38

opera, although of course she's not that heavy, I suppose it's her pink, and that hair. Anyway, she must have something he can't pass up even though she left him flat. But what about Jill?''

"She told me—and said for God's sake don't tell *him*—that she thought she could swing it by Christmas. He'd been too lazy to get a divorce but she's pushing him and he wasn't putting up any objections, just said he hadn't gotten around to it.''

"April in Paris, you can keep it,'' Jill Gaynor said, and cut her visit to her sister short by a week. It was bone-chillingly cold and rainy. There had been, in her ten days there, one morning of sunshine.

Besides, she explained to her sister, she had a pot boiling on the stove back home, and must see to it, the pot being Harley.

She was a woman in her late thirties who broke the married-and-divorced pattern among the gentry of Mute; she had lived with the men of her choice since she was seventeen, and had always lived very well. She thought Harley would make a marvelous and suitable windup to her wanderings.

Permanence, all of a sudden, looked good to her. Money, the getting of it, had begun to be a bore. She had a little of her own and three years back had bought into a thriving antiques and curiosity shop in Brookfield Center; working there had been fun for a while, you met everybody, there was usually an unofficial small party going on in the back office.

It had just started to pall—she was by nature lazy—when she met Harley at Mike Heard's and they fell into, without any dithering about it, a passion for each other. That had been eight months ago. She didn't move into his house, not for any fear of the public tongue, but because for right now she liked her own small old pink brick on Main Street, with the garden behind; and at times wanted great soft seas of privacy.

But they were to all intents and purposes a pair, a union.

As always after the eight-hour flight back—when you took off from Orly at one-thirty and arrived eerily at Kennedy at five-thirty—she had a drink and a sandwich in her room at the Plaza and put herself to bed. Late the next morning, using the transportation arrangements of the better-heeled residents of

Mute, she took a helicopter from Wall Street to the Mute airport.

It would be fun to surprise Harley, appear when he thought she was still three thousand miles away. He himself took a puckish delight in surprises, especially when they unnerved people.

Home, she unpacked, changed her clothes, and drove to his house. Delightfully different weather here, a proper late April. Warm and soft, the trees pale drifts of green, the air like satin against the skin, the sun a blessing.

It was close to two; he'd be surfacing soon, coming out for his drinks and his lunch. She left her car where it couldn't be seen from the house, parked in front of the stand of birchwoods between Herkimer Road and the green semicircle of the house lawn, and strolled up the drive.

The french windows of the living room were open. She walked in through the one nearest the front door and stopped just inside and looked at Marta Ross, sitting on the sofa.

Nothing could have been more peaceful, settled, domestic, than the picture, somehow outside of time, that hit her, froze her.

Embroidery hoop in the woman's hand. Afternoon sun from the window on her hair. An open book on the cushion beside her, a tall drink—the lime quarter proclaimed it as gin and tonic—on the lilac marble-topped coffee table.

It was Marta who spoke first. "Jill . . . Gaynor, isn't it? I think I bought a piece of lovely old silver at your nice shop. A Boston caudle cup."

Serene, blast her, neither welcoming nor unwelcoming. Very much, goddamn her, the lady of the house.

Feeling winded, and as though she had been kicked in the stomach, Jill gathered herself together. "Just what the hell are you doing here?"

Marta studied her assessingly. Tall, lithe. Careless billowing mane of lion-colored hair, long flashing dark eyes under imperiously drawn eyebrows. High-bridged nose with flaring nostrils, wide sensuous mouth now tense with astonished rage. The word pretty had nothing to do with her but she would be attractive, desirable—very, Marta supposed, to a man who was not put off by the hot temper and strong will the cut of the nostrils conveyed, the air about her which her mother would call *sauvage*.

Evidently Harley hadn't been put off by these qualities. Evidently Jill Gaynor felt she belonged here; that this territory was staked out for her.

To the question, she answered mildly, "I live here. If I remembered you, you may remember me? I'm Mrs. Ross, Marta Ross."

The other woman's eyes dismissed her as an outrageous mistake of vision: someone not really there at all. She stalked lion-haired head high, across the room and into the hall and then Marta heard the fist on the door of Harley's workroom, pounding.

Harley's greeting was an appalled "Oh, Christ *no*." He was sitting at his desk at his ominously silenced typewriter. He got up very slowly, something of the invalid about his tall powerful body, and she thought he was backing away from her. But, no, he was standing still.

"What is that woman doing here, that great blond complacent barefooted squatting beast," Jill, running her words together, demanded.

He sighed and said, "I thought you were safely in Paris for a while, I forgot how long. . . ."

"Are you drunk, or crazy, or which? Or both? Have you lost your senses? What is she *doing* here?"

Harley gestured helplessly at the door to indicate that Marta might be listening outside it. Helpless!—big dominating Harley, striding his world laureled with success and money, gulping down life with thirsty glee, almost always unable to wait to make love to her the moment she came near him after even a short separation.

He took her hand and led her to a window opposite the door, thirty feet from it. He whispered, "Can't talk now."

"What do you mean, can't talk, who's she to stop it?" Jill cried. "Doesn't she know that *I am your woman?*"

Still holding her hand—she had never felt his palm cold and damp before—he went to his desk. He sat down and typed, on the sheet of blank paper in the typewriter: "Quiet down and I'll give you a drink. Then for God's sake go home and I'll be

over later, I'm not exactly sure when. Something's come up."
In caps, he added, "TEMPORARILY." He laughed a low
bitter laugh and murmured, "Do you know, these are the very
first useful functional sentences I've gotten down this morning?"

Still deeply alarmed, she sat down and accepted her martini.
Cheering in a small way that he mixed and drank them in here,
now, not as always before out in the living room. Obviously
not eager for the company of that woman.

"I live here."

In a voice almost normal except that it had lost its vital
bounce, Harley asked, raising his glass, "How was Paris? Not
good I gather, you're home early." His head was seething; he
had prepared a number of explanations to give her when she
turned up, all of which sounded even to him, given to flights
of the imagination, quite mad.

Sometime later today he'd have to offer her one that went
down and stayed down, or else. Another cyclone center besides
the occupant of the living room.

She sat tensed, bent forward, in her lean black pants and a
tangerine pongee shirt that she had demanded of him. Her
shoulders were broad, and the shirt almost fitted; she had tied
the tails at her waist. He felt her eyes exploring his hands, his
face, furiously trying to find the answer to an impossible puzzle.

"Rainy. Freezing. Ghastly." She ground the words out between her teeth; a safe-sounded vent for rage. She finished her
drink in two gulps and stood up. "I don't want to play this
particular game, here, any longer, it's a bore. I'll hope to see
you shortly. After all your day's work is over."

She opened the door into the long wide center hall of the
house, walked down it and out the front door, without a glance
into the living room. From it she heard what sounded like a
contented tinkle of ice cubes.

Dove, holding Custard, was sitting on the dry stone wall in
front of the birches. Jill stopped and said, "Hello, Dove, why
aren't you in school?"

"Teachers' convention. Hello, Mrs. Gaynor." She felt some
kind of blast coming from the tall woman, like fireplace heat.

No doubt, Jill thought, her own friends would all be too

eager to supply her with details of the presence here of Marta Ross; but Dove, at the source, was too good an opportunity to pass up.

"Tell me about Mrs. Ross. Why is she here, when did she arrive, how long is she staying?"

Taking the questions in turn, Dove said, "I don't know why, he went off like a—" His reaction had reminded her of the noise the panel truck had made last fall, when its back had tilted up and two cords of wood came thundering and crashing to the ground; but she thought that was too complicated to go into—"well, you know how he is. She got here, around noon, last Friday. Then two great big trunks came. Aunt Em unpacked them. She wonders too, about how long—she says there are clothes for all year. Boots and furs and things. She has her own room. But she's his wife?" Her clear eyes were questioning and a little troubled under the blown brown silky hair.

She left out the sounds, the words from the workroom, "Christ almighty, I won't have it—" and the jagged sob, even though the memory still vividly disturbed her. It didn't seem fair, somehow. Telling on him.

It would have been nice if Jill Gaynor could have explained Mrs. Ross to *her*.

"Husbands and wives do have their fallings out, but in ways this house is like an armed camp," her aunt had observed, almost to herself, as she shared Dove's morning cocoa.

Harley sat at his typewriter motionless, but as though unable to leave its distressingly silent company.

Thrusting Jill aside—deliberately slamming a mental door; one insoluble problem at a time was enough to deal with—he thought, try again to buy her off? Up the ante to maybe thirty thousand? God, no, if I had to earn that before I made a penny for myself, I might dry up completely. Not that I'm dried up now, not at all, it's just a matter of adjusting. Inside this room everything is as it always was, I'm alone, I'm free—

I'll sell this big comfortable house out from under her and find some broken-down hut in Siasconset or far out on Long Island or in some dismal forgotten town in Maine, that she wouldn't want to set foot in. Already he felt the rain from a leak in the roof dripping onto the back of his neck and splashing his electric typewriter. His hands on the keys . . . Suddenly, famous novelist Harley Ross, at his secluded home in . . . Electrocuted while at work.

I'll leave the house and her in it, get an apartment in New York, work there, live there. What's to stop her moving in with me, in New York?

I'll offer her a long holiday abroad, London, Florence, Tangiers, damn the expense. "Lovely, if you'll come with me, Harley."

Maybe I can find her another man. Put her up on the block. She's still a good-looking woman, perhaps she'll tire of this act, if I make it so unpleasant for her that her daily life will become unbearable.

But, my dear chap, she's the one who's holding the cards, not you. More accurately, she has you by the balls. As far as making things unpleasant, impossible, inescapable, for someone.

By God I'll—

His mind stopped there, not able to pronounce to itself the words, the deed.

SEVEN

"My, you're . . . tigerish," Jill said, rolling contentedly away from him and reaching for cigarettes on the bedside table.

"Compliment, if it is one, returned. While you're at it, light two."

After a few luxurious silent minutes, she turned her head on the pillow and looked into his large half-closed blue eyes, "Now. I've held my peace and held my tongue, first things first, but tell me about that woman. Tell me what she's doing there, embroidering and drinking gin in your living room."

"You probably called ten people before I got here and asked them about it," Harley said. "What did they tell you?"

"That . . ." The tightening curve of her upper lip against her teeth looked dangerous. "The two of you have been reunited, she's here to stay. Not, to them, a nine-days' wonder, perhaps a one-day wonder."

"And do you believe that?"

"No."

Harley, exhaling smoke, said slowly and deliberately, to the celing, "She's in trouble. She's done something she shouldn't have done. She asked, plainly and simply, for shelter, for a short time. This business of our getting back together is simply a face-saving cover-up." Yes, it was going quite well, he thought, as gratified as when his typewriter had discovered sentences he didn't know were in his head. "She has some money coming through, something to do with a property of her father's that's in the process of being sold, and then she'll be moving on."

It gave him great pleasure to have Marta guilty, Marta on the run, Marta asking for shelter, for favors.

A wide smile that he was unaware of vanished as Jill said, "I don't believe a word of it. You're too self-centered, self-willed, to let anyone take you over in that way, use you. I can see you doing it to someone else but I can't imagine you on the receiving end."

Write another paragraph. "Look, it's not a question of her taking me over. I could raise hell and do battle but it would get in the way of my work. I prefer to save my energies for that. There's nothing left between us, nothing at all, in fact I can't stand the sight of her. But it won't be for long."

"Have you any idea of what's happened to you? You're *inside* . . . but have you seen yourself from the outside? You look, God help us, as if you've caught something fatal."

Calmly, "I'm having trouble with the book. A disease I can count on at least twice a year." But he was terrified. If she could see it, the beginning of destruction, could everybody else? Get a tan, his furiously racing mind commanded. Swim in the fountain pool every day no matter how cold the water is. Start taking vitamins. Maybe a quart of milk every night before he went to bed, instead of all that scotch?

"Wild as it sounds, it's almost as if that bitch had something on you," Jill said, allowing a little space to fall between each word. "Or has made you think she has. You fiction types are ridiculously prone to fall for other people's fictions."

Don't react. Don't even blink. He turned away from her to put his cigarette out in the ashtray, composed his face, turned back, raised himself on his elbow and looked down at her, wearing his enormous merry grin.

"Jill darling. Leave the fiction to me, you're obviously no good at it. One, I've told you why she's here. Two, if you repeat it, a word of it, to anyone, I will never see you again."

Now a note of plaintiveness entered the ringingly hard voice. "Will you be a good girl and help instead of making things worse? And for Christ's sake shut up about it?"

He had for a second or so frightened her. Big and naked and not a foot away. Her bones had seemed to melt and she wanted to snatch the sheet up over her, for some kind of protection.

Something had almost leaped at her, something had almost struck.

"All right," she said, surprised by the frailty of her own voice. And then, rallying, unused to taking orders from men, even from Harley, "But it damned well better be a short time."

It was six o'clock when he got home. Marta was—the spider enthroned in its web, he thought—comfortably settled in the living room, brimming martini in front of her, music on, Gounod, the ballet suite from *Faust*.

"Just in the nick," she said. "Actually, I was waiting for you. I'll fix yours for a change."

As though it was any man, any wife, any cocktail hour. She had on a long blue dress, slit to the knees in front, showing the shapely sturdy pink calves. The blue was, probably not by accident, the exact color of her eyes.

"Thanks, no, I prefer my own," he said, walking to the painted dresser. To his back, she said thoughtfully, "You've been to that Gaynor woman. . . ." making the words "been to" sound peculiarly obscene.

Feeling the knots of rage tying themselves in his stomach again, he mixed English gin and the unassuming California vermouth he liked, stirred ice cubes, and carefully poured.

Still with his back to her, he said, "I seem to remember you saying, I won't interrupt your way of life at all."

"Of course I meant your home life, your work. Do give me the front of you and not the back, Harley . . . this is important."

He sat down in the wing chair. Two dangerous women, one right after the other were, he thought, two too many.

"People know it's part of your normal pattern, carrying on, extramarital bits and pieces," Marta explained. "But just at the start, the new start, of us, it looks a little peculiar. It sort of makes our whole scheme seem to fall on its face."

Our whole scheme.

"Are you quite mad?" He remembered Jill asking him something like that, a few hours back.

"No, just the opposite. Being sensible for both of us." She let that hang in the air, picked up her drink and took a relishing sip. "For the time being I don't think you should see any more

of . . . what is it, Fran? Lily? . . . Gaynor. Except socially,
of course.''

Mrs. Nairn's comfortable working arrangements included
weekends off. Normally she stayed there, in what she thought
of as almost her own home, and Dove's; getting her garden
started, reading, lazing, teaching Dove how to cook and sew,
lessons her niece enjoyed.

But this April Saturday morning, after guiding Dove through
the making of a frothy satiny white icing with fresh lemon juice
in it, and approving her spreading of it, on three layers of the
cooled fragrant cake, she said:

"I think we both need a change. We'll go see your Aunt
Grace in Danbury, will we? Spend the night.''

Dove said yes, she'd like to. Aunt Grace was Mrs. Nairn's
sister-in-law, a roly-poly woman of radiantly good temper, who
had a daughter Dove's own age, and nice.

There were all sorts of things wrong in the Ross house,
things you couldn't always put your finger on.

The heavy silences at the dinner table (Mrs. Nairn didn't
serve but did put her very good food over hot plates on the
buffet). Up to a little while ago, Harley had been a cheerful
funny fountain of conversation as she came and went, with
aromatic salads, and coffee, and dessert. "Do have some, Mr.
Ross, it's not fattening, peaches and grapes and a touch of
honey and brandy, done in the blender. Full of nutrients, I
should think.''

And then, the feeling that it was no longer his house, but
wholly Mrs. Ross's, although she didn't in any way interfere
with Mrs. Nairn's routine. She was invariably amiable, with
the easy politeness of one brought up with maids and cooks
and gardeners.

And the look of *him,* an exuberant balloon pricked, the air
somehow gone out of it, although his measurements, his height
and breadth, were the same. He wasn't good, Mrs. Nairn be-
lieved, at keeping things to himself. Now and then she would
catch on his face a look that if she wasn't an understating sort
of woman she would call anguish. And then, those terrifying

bouts of rage with his book, his shouting from the workroom echoing through the house, his awful language. "Put your hands over your ears, Dove."

Was it his book he was really shouting at? Or was it his wife, even though she wasn't in there with him.

It all gave her the feeling she had when she was out in the garden, and there was something on the stove, and she kept alert to the moment before which it might boil over and flood her clean white porcelain stovetop.

Harley saw her going down the drive in her modest small black Chevrolet. He was sitting reading his *Times* in the living room. Funny, he thought, a man can read his newspaper just as if his world hadn't come crashing around his ears. Look at me, country squire. Saturday tweeds. A pleasant odor drifting up to his nose from his body. Puig's Agua Lavanda, imported from Spain, palmed on after his morning shower.

It dawned on him that for the first time since she'd come back, the house was empty. Mrs. Nairn had as a courtesy informed him of her weekend plans, and Marta had driven to Westport to buy clothes and have lunch with friends there.

He put down his newspaper, yawned, stretched, and without conscious volition found that his feet were starting him quietly up the stairs.

He went first into her room, standing in the center of it, feeling it full of her, crowded with her. He opened the top drawer of the graceful white dresser and stood looking into its partitioned sections. Neat woman, always had been. He picked up a long scarf, one of folded dozens, this of mauve silk taffeta that whispered as he ran his hands along it, stretching his arms wide until the scarf was taut. To an invisible salesperson, he said aloud, "Just looking, thank you."

He examined her medicine cabinet next. Yes, she still had her sleeping pills, a nearly full bottle of them. According to the label, the prescription had been filled by a druggist in Charleston, South Carolina. She had, he recalled, bouts of insomnia once or twice a year, otherwise never touched them.

He crossed the landing to his own room, opened the double closet doors and fingered thoughtfully one of the sixty or so ties on the triple racks. "Something of a dandy, that fellow Ross is," he informed the air. "You remember Ross, used to be a writer."

God, am I going a little nutty? No, I have always talked to myself out loud, always will, it's entirely normal for me.

In his own medicine cabinet, there was a bottle of tranquilizers. He'd had occasion to resort to them in the last seven days but there must be, oh, seventy-five or so left. His doctor, knowing Harley's airy way of pill swallowing, had caused to be typed on the label, "Absolutely not more than one a day and never while drinking."

Hanging, for decoration by the window from its strap, was an antique razor with a rosewood handle inlaid with mother-of-pearl. He'd picked it up at a country auction because its fineness and forthright wickedness pleased him. He delicately put a thumb to the edge of the blade. Careful, don't cut yourself. Yes, sharp, very much in business after how many decades?

He went downstairs. Passing the ample open entrance to the living room, the tall paneled white doors folded back, he saw out of the corner of his eye the two heavy Georgian silver candlesticks on the mantelpiece. The two-foot-high, round-bellied, long-necked Waterford crystal vase to the right of the hearth, holding one tall branch of white lilac. The fireplace furniture to the left, shovel, tongs, poker; English, old, brass, a nuisance to polish but then he didn't have to do it. Weighty, handsome, and efficient.

People don't realize, he thought, what arsenals of potentially dangerous weapons ordinary houses are, from pills to pokers. But of course, he told himself, I am just thinking in the abstract. It's nice to be thinking at all again.

It's a good thing they *don't* realize it. Otherwise, given a situation where a person was subjected by another person to unendurable stress for any length of time . . .

"There would be a litter of bodies from here to Bridgeport," he said, and passing an oval mirror on the wall near the kitchen got an unexpected and startling look at his face. As he often did, he wrote about it in his head. "Fey, a little fanatic, or was it satanic?—the blaze of the bulging eyes, intent frown shooting the eyebrows up at the outer ends, the color, over-supplied by the heart, a strong scarlet but not unbecoming, the color of a man still furiously alive. A look of mirth about the mouth, but not mirth that had anything to do with the hidden inner man . . ."

"Have you ever seen yourself from the outside?"

Opening drawers and cabinets, immaculately maintained, in the kitchen, he came on heavy French enameled pots and pans, a wooden potato masher he had never laid eyes on, the Sabatier carbon steel knives, honed blades graduated from eighteen inches to six; an object which he finally identified as a meat hammer, plain wood on one side of its striking head, corrugated metal on the other, a satisfying heft in the hand.

He hadn't seen the meat hammer before, either—had Mrs. Nairn bought it? Or Marta. A man should, like a good house-holder, take occasional inventory of his own possessions.

In a way it was a relief to go out the back door and feel the wind on his hot skin. He turned left when he came to the pool, crossed the gravel driveway and went into the garage.

Kenniston, the man who came twice a week to take care of the lawns and wash windows and do whatever else Mrs. Nairn thought necessary, kept tools there, neatly out of the way of the spaces for the two cars.

A long-handled scythe. Shades of Thomas Hardy, Harley thought. What did he use it for? The meadows, probably, when they got too deep in grass and daisies and buttercups. Three different kinds of hammers, slung over nails on the wall. What did you do with three kinds of hammers? A power mower. A six-foot saw and its three-foot junior, gleaming, oiled. An electric power saw zipped into a thick plastic case. He hated the relentless noise of them but when dead limbs had to be hacked from living trees— Efficient, he supposed.

He was feeling a little lightheaded. Time for a drink, some-thing to eat, and perhaps start that tan, but first he felt a great need of air, and space, and freedom from himself.

To get to the top of the almost sheer bluff at the back of the house, you had to go through the upward-tilting apple orchard at its left side, swing right again and climb the precipitous path between birch and spruce trees. The cowardly and lazy had been known to help themselves up the path by grasping holes and branches.

He walked in the high windiness to the edge of the bluff, to where the waterfall, which had its origin in an underground spring in the lifting heights behind him, sprang fiery white and silver from just below the lip.

Dizzying, watching the plunge of the water. Move back, it urges you to follow it, makes your head feel odd . . . but all it does, really, is meet itself safely, in celebration, in foam and music, all the way down there, below.

It must be fifty feet down, the pool. As apartment buildings were, meanly, built today, that would be approximately five floors or a little over.

A square slate terrace on the side of the pool opposite the garage, about thirty-five feet across. It looked handsome from up here, and very far below, and very hard. Thank God he hadn't had to pay for it. It had been here when he bought the house.

EIGHT

Feeling he had emerged from a peculiar and unpleasant dream, during which he walked in his sleep, roamed strange dark places, Harley reached for routine, for comfort.

He made himself a martini and then, before sitting down to drink it, rashly decided to take a quick look through the checkbook, a hardbound affair with three checks to a page. It was kept in the green lacquer desk.

Ann Tree, $700. Repayment of a loan, obviously. Self, $500. To a doctor he'd never heard of—New York?—$220. Again, self, $175.

He bitterly grudged her every penny of it. He felt a pounding in his temples and knew without a mirror that the veins there were showing themselves. For God's sake, drink your drink.

The phone rang. An efficient female voice: "Confirming Mrs. Ross's appointment for Monday at ten with Doctor Ventnor." Naturally she'd choose the most expensive dentist in the county, a New York man who'd found the practice up here even more lucrative. Harley himself used him, easier than the trek to New York, and in the past year had rolled up fees of over a thousand dollars in the comfortable colonial offices.

Goddamn it, even when she wasn't here, she was here.

The phone rang again. " 'arley!" Marta's mother Berthe, with whom he had not exchanged a word in two years. He made a neutral noise and she said, "Congratulations, dear. I do think it's so wise and sensible of both of you, at your ages." She made no attempt to keep the chuckling malice out of her voice.

What explanation had Marta given her? *Or could she know the whole thing and need no explanation?* Probably not, though—Marta disliked and distrusted her mother.

He put the back of his wrist to a sweating forehead and said, "Sorry, Berthe, can't talk, I'm in the midst of a mess of overdue galleys—"

"Sorry to disturb the great man," Berthe said. "But I did want you to know how pleased I am that she's safely settled and cared for again. I loved your last book—what was the title?—it's slipped my mind, but you did let me down awfully in the last chapter, maybe you were in a rush then, too, finishing it? Goodbye, my happily retrieved son-in-law. Give Marta my regards."

He stood looking at his empty glass. Then he hurled it into the fireplace. Being Val. St. Lambert crystal, it smashed musically and dramatically, sending a glistening shower back onto the rug.

Returning at a little after five, Marta asked, "What's that glass all over the rug in front of the fireplace?"

"I was toasting my retrieved wife, in the Russian fashion," Harley said. The suppressed violence in his voice gave her pause.

"Why hasn't Mrs. Nairn cleaned it up?"

"For the first time in months, Mrs. Nairn and the kid have fled this happy home for a weekend elsewhere. She took exception to a request of mine that she put rat poison in your after-dinner Brie."

"Oh, Harley, for God's sake."

Talking wildly, grotesquely, wasn't new to him; he liked to play with the language, sometimes very darkly.

But the overt threat with its hard edge of laughter, the broken glass—he must have thrown it with all his strength, he must have been consumed with rage—bothered her as she went up the stairs to bathe and change.

He wouldn't . . . *do* anything to her, would he?

She had been prepared in reinstating herself as his wife for verbal violence, sulks, storms, tantrums, which she told herself would in time die away, he wouldn't want to disturb the steady stream of his work. But never, in their worst quarrels, had he so much as laid a finger on her; it was all noise, bulging eyes, and furious color.

Deep in hot water, she relaxed and allowed herself a rosier view. He was an extremely intelligent man. Sooner or later they'd be back on a calm amiable footing, comfortable for both. He'd see that there was just no other way to live his life. He had an enormous appetite for pleasure, gaiety, laughter.

Yes, he'd adapt. There was nothing else for him to do.

The very qualities which had once made her his rock, his restful center now became, moment to moment, more detestable. Her serenity (for that read complacency, he said to himself; unimaginative cow). Her calm silences (she never had and never will have any conversation worth listening to). Her firm protecting of him from intrusions, nuisances, mind-scattering matters (it's like having a policewoman in residence).

He never worked on Saturdys or Sundays unless on galleys, which he considered strawberries and cream after the task of writing the damned thing. He walked his fast three or four miles in all seasons. Summers, he played tennis with Mike Heard, swam in the pool at the Mute Country Club or in Blessing Lake half a mile from his house, went to late lazy lunches, and pool and cocktail parties. Winters, he skated and skied, entertained around his own blazing hearth, caught up on his reading, wrote poetry, at which he knew he was very bad. At all seasons he played poker on nights when he found willing victims.

This rainy Sunday, he went at seven-thirty to his workroom just as, he thought, a livery horse to its stable. Privacy for six hours or so, peace if you could call it that, because she wasn't in his sight or hearing. In one week, he had written only seven useful pages, and these only when he'd allowed himself morning scotch and too many cigarettes. His normal output would have been forty-eight or fifty pages.

Now, today, he didn't even try. He lay on his sofa and half slept, rousing himself after a while to read, without attention, the Sunday *Times*.

I'm a faulty tap that's been turned off, he thought, all you can hear is a small maddening drip, drip. . . .

When he emerged for his drinks and lunch, Marta said. "Just two calls. John McIndoe, he'll call back tonight. And that woman, I've got her name straight, Jill. I said you were working and of course couldn't be disturbed, and was there any message, and she said no."

What Marta had said to Jill was: "He can't be bothered." And then after the slightest pause, "I mean, I can't interrupt him."

As well as a quick scald of rage, Jill felt a consuming curiosity about the Ross menage. She considered a moment, and then picked up the phone and called Polly Ingram.

Always direct, she said without preliminaries, "I want to see Harley, but if I go over alone the woman probably won't let me into the house. Will you two form a flying wedge for me? We'll take them by surprise."

"Love to," Polly said. "He's been declining invitations right and left, including ours. I'm dying to see the happy pair again. Lucky Marta, talk about falling on your feet!"

Sorely tempted, Jill held her tongue.

"Too marvelous," Polly said to her husband, Bob. "To see wife and best girl face to face!"

Opening the door to them, Marta was for a split second openmouthed in surprise and displeasure. To Polly, she said, "How nice, on a rainy day."

"Should have called," Polly said, "but we were just passing by and thought what fun to disturb the Rosses' peace and quiet."

Harley heard the voice and thankfully shouted from the living room, "Welcome one and all, whoever you are," and as they went in stopped dead, his greeting hand held out, his eye falling on Jill.

She walked over to him and kissed his jaw lightly. Silence, a crash of it. The only sound to be heard was the delightful noise of the waterfall.

Jill looked around and laughed. "What's all this about? Hasn't anyone ever seen a lady kiss her feller?" She reached into the pocket of her ivory whipcord pants. "I brought your watch along, darling. You forgot to put it back on the other day."

Eyes went to Harley's wrist, where the was a stripe of paler skin on the beginning tan.

"Thank you," Harley said formally, not daring at the moment to put it on because they would enjoy the spectacle of his shaking hands.

Poor man, Polly Ingram thought, to blush so violently, or, she supposed, with men it was called flushing.

"And now, what are we all drinking?" Harley asked.

Marta had resumed her seat on the sofa during the kiss. Polly thought her composure a little frightening. It was Jill who looked off keel, dark eyes blazing, swift hand combing through her lion's hair.

"Irish for us," Bob said. "We've taken a fancy to it. If you have it."

"We have it," Jill said.

"A martini for you, Harley, of course, and for me," Marta said. "Nothing for Ms. Gaynor. I will not have her in my house. The sooner we narrow our circle the pleasanter."

Jill, standing, rested an elbow on the mantelpiece. "*Your* house. Difficult to get used to—last I heard it was Harley's."

Harley, the articulate, the fountain of words, said almost under his breath, "Now . . . look here . . . Marta, Jill . . ."

"Oh, honestly, Marta," Polly said, "everybody kisses everybody these days, everybody's 'darling' to everybody—"

"What the hell are you trying to explain away?" Jill cried. "We all know where Harley and I stand." She went over to him and put an arm about his taut waist.

Marta got up from the sofa and moving swiftly slapped her face with a large and heavy hand. Jill reeled back, recovered herself, dove, and in the fragment of a second had Marta on the floor, tearing at her braided chignon.

Harley allowed Marta several screams of pain.

In a strange way, the sight of the two battling, writhing women on the rug seemed to ease, vicariously, some awful tightness inside him.

Then he bent and seized a handful of Jill's black linen shirt and hauled her to her feet. Bob Ingram reached down a helping hand to Marta, whose braids had come loose and were swinging to her waist in back.

"Now then," Harley said. "Will both of you please stop panting? Jill, you and I will retire to my room for a quiet drink, it appears that you two"—he gave Marta a long look—"are not compatible. I'm sure our guests will excuse us."

(Bob Ingram didn't dare voice it then, but remembered it later for Polly. "Separate but equal," he said.)

"Marta, I had no idea your hair was so long," Polly managed. And, "Would you be happier without us?"

"No, where were we, oh, just ordering drinks. Bob, will you take over?" She looked like a large Dutch doll, with her braids loose and the brilliant rose patches under her clear blue eyes. Between clenched white teeth, she said:

"Well, it's no news to any of his friends that Harley likes to live dangerously."

"I haven't enjoyed myself so much since I kicked my gym teacher," Jill said. "Did you hear the whack when her head hit the floor? She'll have a colossal lump."

"My sweet," Harley said, pouring scotch, "I'm on your side but you both asked for it."

In his head, as was his habit, he composed a sentence.

"Polly Ingram, after the shocked tears dried, said, 'Ghastly as it is—poor *Marta*—anyone seeing them there on the floor would know that Jill wanted to kill her.' "

NINE

"Why do people live together if they don't like each other?" Dove asked, and then, correcting herself, "At least he doesn't like her."

With the view of getting in strong moral points before Dove was old enough and wise enough to question them, Mrs. Nairn said, "Well, first and foremost, they happen to be married."

Dove was in the middle of an ironing lesson and she looked thoughtfully at the shirt cuff.

"Permanent press is all very well," Mrs. Nairn had instructed, starting her off. "But you do bump into pure unadulterated cotton here and there and you're better off knowing how to handle it. Now. Collar first, yoke next, then the two sleeves and cuffs, then the back, and finally the left and right sides of the front."

"Why?"

"So you won't wrinkle what's gone before." It was one of those skilled certainties of her aunt's that Dove found so comforting in an increasingly mysterious world.

She was practicing on a pink pima cotton shirt of Harley's. Mrs. Nairn was making cream sauce, with sherry and grated Gruyere, for the filet of flounder; the little green grapes would be dropped in at the last minute. Relenting as she whisked— after all, Dove was bright, no point in talking down to a bright child, pushing them back instead of helping them forward—she added, "At your age you know that people aren't always the way you expect them to be."

Dove, carefully ironing a pocket, decided that she would

devote herself wholly, in the next few days, to finding out. In the matter of Harley and Mrs. Ross. Why?

Once you knew why, everything became all right, acceptable. You wouldn't get odd disturbing dreams in the night. Like Harley using her braided chignon for a croquet ball, smashing his mallet at it, driving it through the two final hoops to hit the stake.

You could turn your attention to the bursting spring, to your birthday and your father's visit two weeks away, and to the kittens poor eight-months-old Custard was going to have.

"Must have her spayed, this is her first time *and* her last," Mrs. Nairn said. "I didn't know there was a tomcat in miles."

Except for weekends, she would only have the afternoons after school for her investigations, but that was enough. He was in his room in the mornings and Mrs. Ross never got up before ten.

Once embarked upon her quest, Dove was intent, determined, and unhampered by what her aunt would call Manners. In three days, she collected quietly—listening, anxious, and unseen— one monologue and two conversations.

Custard had returned to her new favorite place under the honeysuckles at one of the west windows of Harley's work-room. Dove went and sat down beside her, close against the sun-warmed stone house wall.

His voice, near, startled her. ". . . a lizard of a boy, quick, dark, flickering, and forward-pointing." Not the way you would talk on the phone, there was a browsing sound to his voice, as if he was reading aloud something he had written. "He occupied his free hours with random, pointless violence. One day a haystack casually fired, the next aiming his speeding motorcycle at a cat strolling across the road—"

Dove put her hands over her ears and felt a thump of pain and outrage in her stomach. After a few seconds, she removed her hands, the cat part ought to be over.

Harley laughed and said in quite a different voice, "Imagine finding him, right here on page eighteen." There was no answer to this, so he must have been talking to himself.

"Harley and Mr. Ross have great conversations with each

other,'' Mrs. Nairn was given to saying.

It would be better if it was just in a book, words on paper, but the lizard boy reminded her of someone. She thought hard and then placed herself and Mrs. Nairn in Meyer's Hardware Store, where her aunt was pricing a roll of nylon twine. Mr. Meyer was occupied with another customer and he shouted toward the back of the store, where the stockroom door was open, ''Get yourself back in here quick, service wanted!''

The boy looked exactly as Harley had described him; about nineteen, maybe, Dove thought. He was polite enough, behind the counter, but there was something about his expressionless dark eyes on her that made Dove want to look away from him.

His customer attended to, Mr. Meyer strolled out to the sidewalk with them, evidently wanting to complain. ''Help, these days, hopeless,'' he said. ''That boy in there, Em, smoking God knows what in the back room, turns up when he feels like it, sometimes not at all—drifts from job to job to pick up money to buy a motorcycle, gas station before he landed on me, and when I can find someone else it's drift again, heaven help his next employer, but with my bad hip I'll stick it out a little longer.''

What did Mr. Ross mean, he'd found him? Found him for what?

As if in partial answer, Harley said, ''If I need him, or anyone, that is. At this point I'm just . . .'' A long pause. ''But if I ever saw anyone who was totally expendable . . .''

After that there was silence.

''What does expendable mean?'' Dove asked Mrs. Nairn.

As always, Mrs. Nairn directed, ''Look it up in the dictionary.''

Dove did. ''Capable of being expended; specif., *Mil.*, normally used up or consumed in service; hence, left in the path of the enemy and sacrificed according to plan, in order to gain time, esp. in a delaying action.'' She went just above this to the word expend. ''To consume by use in any way; to use up; to spend.''

It was puzzling; the boy wasn't in the army, but for some reason Harley thought he could be used up and spent.

*　　*　　*

Voices from the kitchen, Dove on her hands and knees fingering nasturtium seeds into the earth. Not too early for them, they're hardy, Mrs. Nairn had said, and, always ready with useful information, added that those very seeds were called capers in caper sauce.

Mrs. Ross. ". . . high time we did some entertaining. People will think it's funny that we don't—you with your overflowing festive board."

"Nonesense, they know we're lost in the raptures of rediscovery." It was Dove's first lesson in how you could say one thing and mean, chillingly, the exact opposite. Harley's words were like thrown stones.

After a little stinging silence, Mrs. Ross: "We'll say next Saturday, shall we? Or perhaps Sunday brunch, depending on availabilities. We'll start with the Hydes, I'd like to get to know them better."

"Are you planning Jill for your list?"

"No. Don't you know she is undermining your safety?"

"It occurred to me the other day that there's no such thing as safety," Harley said. "I was wandering through the house and around my demesne and you have no idea what an arsenal we live in. Knives, hammers, scythes . . ." He laughed, but Dove didn't know why. "It's a good thing, isn't it, that we're civilized people."

"Oh, do stop shaking verbal fists at me." Her tone was safe and settled, and a little impatient; what Dove called wife's-voice. "I know it's only your way of saber rattling, but . . . if anything did ever happen, along the lines of your inflamed imaginings, remember it's the spouse the police always look to first. Naturally."

A little noise as the refrigerator door was opened. "That divine Mrs. Nairn read my mind, melon and prosciutto. Are you as hungry as I am?"

Driven back to the dictionary, Dove looked up "arsenal." "A public establishment for making and storing arms and military equipment; hence, figuratively, a storehouse."

Arms. She looked at her own, thin and already delicately tanned. Storehouses full of them, detached from bodies . . . No, weapons were what they meant by the word, guns, rifles, cannons, to kill people with, that's what were stored in arsenals.

She thought it was nice that, according to the kitchen clock, her aunt would soon get up from her Sunday nap.

Mrs. Nairn made a small involuntary sound suggesting indigestion, and said, "Run down and get me the bicarbonate of soda, left-hand cabinet over the sink. My eggplant isn't sitting quite right."

It was close to ten o'clock, which was Dove's bedtime. She went down the boxed-in back stairway to the kitchen. It wasn't a matter of half-eavesdropping this time; it was impossible not to hear, and be distressed by, the voice from the living room. Thick. Heavy with, what was it, grief?

("He's drinking too much, that's not like him, usually holds it like a general," Mrs. Nairn said.)

". . . Christ, John, I feel as if I'd been walking across a nice safe flat plain and fell down a well, or an abandoned mine shaft, all the way down. Can you hear me from the bottom of it? Am I coming through at all?" A short silence while someone at the other end of the telephone conversation presumably talked. And then, "Don't make me laugh. Seven pages in seven days, I don't dare read them or I'd throw them away . . . and, no, I can't offer you an explanation, my lips, as they say, are sealed. Suffice it to add that I wish I were dead. Now that I've ruined your evening—have another drink, Harley. But *you* were the one who called me, that's right. . . . No, if I go on I'll say things that can't be said. Good night."

TEN

"My Star of India," John McIndoe said distractedly. "My Bank of England. My Fort Knox. Can't *work!* It's never happened before, the man's a machine."

He was addressing his partner, Anny Adams, in the firm of McIndoe and Adams Literary Agency. Their offices were on the parlor floor of an ample brownstone overlooking Stuyvesant Square, tall airy rooms with floor-to-ceiling windows, plaster garlands overhead, elegant marble fireplaces.

John's first thought after last night's eerie conversation with Harley was that his client might have contracted some terrible disease, or at least thought he had. He had tendencies to hypochondria coupled with a terror of doctors. "Of course they'll find something wrong with you if you go to them," he said. "That's what their business is all about."

But then, why, in sinister antique fashion, had he said that his lips were sealed? He was usually given to pouring out symptoms in full and colorful detail.

Hands in his pockets, head bent, impatiently striding the dimmed old flame and rose Persian rug, he went on, "Shattered. That's what he sounded like. Absolutely shot to hell."

"Writers do have private lives and private problems," Anny pointed out. "If I know Harley it probably has something to do with a woman. Sit down, John, you're making me nervous. No doubt it will all blow over, you just caught him at a bad moment."

She was the optimistic partner; he the pessimist. "It's your dour Scottish blood," she had analysed. He was tall, thin, and

English-tailored, with a narrow bony understanding face and fine slate gray eyes. His father Bernard McIndoe had been a legendary New York publisher who bought the best before anyone knew they were good; lived gaily, creatively, and alcoholically; and died a happy man at the age of fifty-five.

It's nice, Anny thought, regarding him affectionately, when successful men have successful sons. Nice, and rare. Like that dear Heywood Hale Broun.

She often thanked heavens that she was happily married; John was an extraordinary attractive presence to spend every day with.

"I'll try him again at one-thirty," he said, sighing. "He'll be sober then."

"And if he's still strange, why not just go up to Mute and see him?"

"I can't go tramping into his life like the F.B.I.," John said. "He'd heave me out."

He left her to the manuscript she was reading and went back to his own office.

". . . if I go on I'll say things that can't be said."

What would boisterous outpouring Harley find to say that couldn't be said?

He got up in the middle of a late lunch with one of his bread-and-butter mystery writers and called Harley at a little before two. Instead of last night's near despair, he met a ghastly, glassy cheerfulness.

"Talked too much last night, we'd been partying."

"Who? Jill? How is she?" He and Jill had once had a short and interesting pairing up; it was through him that the two had met, at Mike Heard's.

"No," Harley said, still in that fake-hearty voice, not his voice at all. "Marta. Didn't you know? We're back together. Bit of a shakeup, naturally, but I'll settle down to my old pace in a week or so."

This explanation bore no resemblance to last night's cry for help.

"Why don't you come into town, back off from the book, take a short breather, you and I can do some constructive drinking."

"Good idea!" cried Harley unconvincingly. "Can't see my way to it right at the moment but if I do I'll give you a ring."

Yes, two different stories; but the desperation was still there. As well as being his biggest moneymaker, by far, he was after their five-year relationship a friend of sorts for whom John felt a crotchety, amused fondness.

He could push it no further now, on the telephone; but the sense of a depth bomb that had gone off, of an actual personality change (or rather two personalities in twenty-four hours) was alarming.

He waited three days and tried again. Marta's soft calm voice, "John! How nice, how are you?" and after an exchange of chit-chat, "No, sorry, Harley's flat on his back with a terrible cold, he's napping now, I mustn't wake him."

Again, odd. Harley was capable of working in a windstorm of paper tissues, trumpeting and sneezing while the typewriter pounded along. An obvious, the simplest, retreat? Get sick, and then you're really out of business, nothing expected of you by yourself or anybody else, until you get better.

"Come and have a sherry with me, I missed lunch," Anny called from the next room. It was a cold and rainy day and she had lit her fire. A pleasing scent filled the high white room, coming from the crackle and leap of flames. Over the sherry, she said, "It just occurred to me. Didn't you, was it early last year, see a lot of Elizabeth Ross for a while? Surely she'd know what's going on. If anything."

Three times his hand had hovered over to the telephone, to being the act of dialing; three times it had been withdrawn.

They had met at Christmastime at a large noisy party at the Plaza, given by Harley's publishers Faunt and Faunt to celebrate the publication of *A Thunder of Eagles*. She was there with a man whose name John hadn't caught, but several minutes after their eyes met across a space of fifteen feet or so he managed, in a relatively quiet corner, to have her to himself for a while.

Among a number of extremely good-looking, worked-on, showy women, she was to the ordinary eye unremarkable. She had a thin responsive clever face, very white skin, dark shining straight hair that swung when she moved her head, and a mouth that now, and often, he later discovered, looked delicately amused. Her eyes were a deep steady blue. She was, she told him upon being asked, a writer of television commercials at G and R.

Harley, seeing them deep in absorbed conversation, came over, slapped John's shoulder with a force that spilled half his drink, gave Elizabeth an affectionate smacking kiss, approved her bare black dress, said, "I've forgotten what well-breasted women the Rosses are," and then attempted without success to remove John to meet a writer who he thought was ripe for burgling from her agent. "Later," John said. "Elizabeth and I have caviar and things to catch up on."

"Basics," he said, over the caviar. "Are you, at the moment, in the words of my calling, under contract to anyone in particular?"

"Not . . . really. Are you?"

"No. Standard American model, at least in this town—one divorce." He wasn't flippant; there was an ironic, slight downcurve to his mouth.

It began then, was followed by lunch the next day, and proceeded, naturally and happily, full speed ahead.

In April, he went to London to sort out problems of a handful of his British writers, which took a great deal longer than he expected. Several days before he got back, she had to leave for Palm Springs for the filming of a package of four commercials for Braceway Foods, which consumed three and a half weeks.

He made several long-distance calls but someone always seemed to be wanting her for something after the first minute or so. She sounded, and literally was, distant and preoccupied, on her professional mettle. Of course, one must respect a woman's right to do her job—all those highly paid camera crews and models and actors—instead of wasting money murmuring into the telephone.

Molly Carmichael, an early love of his, came over from Dublin for a month. The three met in an embarrassing way, waiting for the light to change at Park Avenue and Thirty-eighth Street. Molly, in her tender, owning fashion, had slipped her arm through his. "Oh, hi," Elizabeth said. "He*llo*," John said.

He called her twice while Molly was still in New York, but she wasn't at home either time. He called her again after Molly left. It had turned into early June. Sorry, honestly, she hadn't the time, she'd gotten involved in things. Gracefully polite and vague.

In the accidental, everyday way, they lost each other.

He never thought of her without a faint guilt and a strong warmth; but he did not take kindly to spurning. Even though the Molly part of it had certainly been his fault.

Now, he thought, the hell with it, stop dithering, business is business, and all that was a long time ago. In the rainy early evening, he called Elizabeth and found her at home.

"Hello, Elizabeth, John McIndoe," and then he swore mentally at himself for the formal addition of his surname. But God knew how many other Johns she had in her life.

She said hello back, pleasantly; he had forgotten how quietly musical her voice was.

"I hope you haven't got a pot boiling over at the moment or company sitting suspended, I wouldn't have bothered you but—" Normally at ease with his own tongue, he thought, God, nice going, a mild insult to himself and to her, simultaneously. *Bothered* you.

In a quick recovery, "To make it brief, it's about Harley."

The unmitigated gall of him, Elizabeth thought, calling after almost a whole year and then in reference to his personal profit.

She was taken aback by the depth of her reaction and the evidence offered by it that John McIndoe—gotten over, filed away, you can't win them all—was still dangerously dear.

"Yes, what about him?" She almost added, "Are his royalties dropping off?" and frightened herself by the shaming near recklessness.

"He's in some kind of bad shape, I've had a few conversations with him this past week. I thought you might know what it was."

Calmly, cooperatively, she said, "I don't see him, you know, more than two or three times a year. As far as I'm concerned there's a stillness, to coin a phrase, from Mute. The last I saw of him he was starting a book tentatively called *Cissie and Caesar*. I think it was about an English duchess and a member of the Mafia. He was as usual happy and excited, reeling off the plot to anyone who'd listen.''

Her ease gave him back his own. "I never thought to ask you before—are you fond of him?''

"Yes, fond is exactly the word, but we're not at all close, never have been. Why?''

"I think he's in trouble and doesn't know how to ask for help.''

"He has friends up there by the barrelful—''

"Family can sometimes spot things that friends can't. I have a quite specific and outrageous favor to ask of you, but I'd prefer to ask it in person.''

"Why not ask now? It will save us both time if my answer is no.'' Again, she was disturbed. Where had the deep anger, a trace of which was leaking out, come from?

"All right. I'd like to drive you to Mute, Saturday or Sunday, and we'd both drop in on him for a friendly drink. I tried to get him to come to New York but he won't.''

"Do you really think it's something that *bad?*''

"I think it's something desperate.''

"Perhaps I should call him, right away, before we—?''

We. Encouraging. For one logical reason and one unexpected, selfish one, he said, "No, that would give him time to put his face on, tidy whatever it is away, for the short spell we'd be there.''

We. Oh well, why not? Harley really might be in need of help.

"I can't go on Saturday, but''—resignedly—"Sunday's all right.''

"Good. I'll pick you up at ten. Is that too early?''

"Not for a long drive. The country,'' she added, in the manner of a person finding some solace to temper an inescapable gray obligation, "ought to be looking pretty now.''

ELEVEN

She was waiting for him, on that bright windy morning, under the canopy of her apartment building on East Seventy-third Street. He startled both of them by coming up to her, bending over, and very lightly kissing her mouth; not unlike husband and wife meeting after a separation of a few hours.

She covered a yawn of nervous reaction as he opened the door of the rented car and she slid in. "Sorry, didn't get to bed until very late, or rather very early."

She was wearing a narrow-waisted emerald green tweed blazer over a Black Watch plaid skirt, the pleats mushrooming as she settled herself. Under the blazer the collar of a white silk shirt showed.

"You look well, anyway," he said, understating. "Would you like to catch up on your sleep until the scenery gets switched on? The Merritt Parkway fails to grab the attention, unless you're driving. Then I'll wake you up."

She had thought it might be difficult, awkward, but saw that it wouldn't be, at all, if she picked up his easy amiability, that of a comfortable, old acquaintance. Old friends often kissed when they met.

"Thank you, I will." She closed her eyes and rolled her head away from him, thinking sleep unlikely, but it would allow for a long natural silence.

No, it wasn't so easy. Unsettling, after a year, to be a foot away from him, on the car seat, to hear and even somehow feel his breathing.

She was aware of a mounting tension in the immediate atmosphere, a crackle. Was he generating it or was she? Wanting

70

air, she wheeled down her window and the wind attacked her hair like a broom. "Oh, hell," she said mournfully, and closed it. She saw him smiling to himself before she reassumed her role as sleeper.

After a while, "Dogwoods tuning up, Elizabeth." She had forgotten the way his tongue lingered over the syllables of her name.

Self-possessed again, she fell into the idle conversation with him as they drove the dappled road between meadows and woods frothed with the pink and white dogwoods. Politics. Books. A play they both liked, a play they had both hated. Mutual friends were not touched upon.

At a little after twelve he pulled the car off the road under a freshly billowing maple. "As the rural inns don't open until one, I brought our lunch. I wanted your errand of mercy to be as comfortable as possible."

Watching him unpack the wicker hamper, and thinking of her own snatched sandwiches and containers of cooling coffee during her daily work, she said, "I'd forgotten what civilized types you literary gentlemen are," and he said, "You've just put the flat of your hand on my chest and given me a good shove backward, Elizabeth, why? I thought I had been being nice and polite."

She blushed in the way he remembered with pleasure, a sudden delectable pink, a widening of the dark blue eyes.

"Sorry, I didn't mean to be bitchy. But as you say, this is an errand, not a . . ."

"It can also be a nice day in the country, to have a reunion on, if you'll relax and allow it to be." He gave her a wrapped golden-brown chicken breast and poured wine as she held the two glasses in her other hand. "I never thought to ask you, are you still Ross?"

"I'm not married, if that's your question."

"Napkins under the pears . . . I could have saved my breath, couldn't I?"

They hadn't gotten around, in those three lovely months, to discussing marriage; they were perfectly happy as they were.

"And you're still McIndoe," she said with her flashing mischievous grin. "Which doesn't indicate anything either. Did you remember the salt?"

                        *   *   *

Well before they began their picnic under the maple, Ms.
Perdita Twinn was preparing to leave her house for the eleven
o'clock service at the Mute Episcopalian Church of St. Andrew.

She was, among other things, a mildly eccentric spinster, a
devoted daughter who had cared for an invalid mother until
death ended this duty last year, and a member of the Church
Guild. But to herself her shining place in her world was being
Mr. Ross's Typist.

To her he entrusted his heavy, untidy manuscripts, knowing
that she would impeccably correct his uncertain spelling, trans-
late his handwritten revisions and annotations—sometimes a
dozen or so to a page—from the almost unreadable scrawl into
crystalline English.

At first, she had thought some of the passages she was typing
were, even for this outspoken day and age a little, well . . .
But Mr. Ross, never Harley to her, was a man of the world,
and after a bit you got used to it, even found a certain guilty
pleasure in it, no one to see your color rising. But that was the
first manuscript, five books back; now she sailed jauntily
through what she called Mr. Ross's Blue Passages.

She adored him, and felt herself an extension of him, and
so identified herself with his work that she couldn't even sleep
a wink the night before *The Wishing Wells* opened at the Mute
motion-picture theater. Tomorrow night she would see Our
Movie. . . .

And just think—pulling on white gloves, checking her neat
blue hat in the hall mirror—our *A Thunder of Eagles* will be
playing here in early June.

Going out of her modest clapboard house, she saw a glimmer
of white in the mailbox by the door. Funny, she'd picked up
her Saturday mail. She slipped the envelope into her handbag
and walked the half mile to church. Arriving as always early,
and having adjusted her kneeler, found the correct place in her
prayer book, ribboned it, and said her own pre-service prayers,
she sat quietly waiting and then remembered the envelope. It
wouldn't hurt to take a discreet peek. Who knows? it might be
something urgent, it must have been hand delivered now that
she thought about it, of course there was no mail delivery on
Sundays.

The envelope face merely said Miss Twinn in inept block printing. There was a sheet of scratch paper inside, folded once. More of the penciled clumsy printing. "I think your employer Mr. Harley Ross ought to know someone is out to get his wife. She came back at the wrong time, she came back to the wrong place, and somebody wants to kill her. It could be that that somebody is you." There was no signature.

A kind of hot darkness buzzed around Perdita Twinn's head.

"Kill Mrs. Ross!" she cried out. "Kill Mrs. *Ross—!*"

The congregation around her was electrified. Heads turned, and then a tide of organ music poured above. Perdita was aware of a kindly arm, a man, it must be the man who had with his wife moved in at the end of the pew just before she opened the envelope.

"It's the heat," the man said, "It's very close in here, come, I'll help you, you need air," and without knowing exactly how she got there, she found herself on the church steps.

Her legs were trembling. She could barely manage the steps as the kind man led her down them, to a stone bench near the church gate, under towering old lilacs.

Then shame and partial recollection straightened her spine. "Thank you. I'll be quite all right, it *was* stuffy. I'll rest a bit and then make my way home, I live just down the road. Thank you so much."

After the service, the kind man's wife said to him, "That was Perdita Twinn. I always thought she was a little touched. It's funny how people like that often let go in church."

Perdita lay on her bed in her darkened room, a handkerchief soaked in lavender eau de cologne on her forehead.

It had come back all too clearly. Her cry or shout, "Kill Mrs. Ross," in the black grasp of astonishment and horror. What would they all think, what would they all say?

Was God punishing her for having carnal thoughts about Mr. Ross? Or wishing Mrs. Ross dead when she, Perdita, was informed that his wife had come back, to stay? On the hearing of which a tiny impossible hope in a lonely breast had sorrowfully expired.

God, she told herself, palms clutching the bedspread, hadn't written a note and left it in her mailbox. The words were real, someone had put them down, she had been merely repeating them.

It was a warning and it must be delivered. How long had she lain here in the near dark? Had she slept? She looked at her watch. Nearly a quarter to one, but it had taken her quite a long time to walk home.

Impelled by a powerful sense of urgency, she rose and bathed her face and tidied her hair. She went downstairs, drank a glass of cold milk, went to the telephone, and called Tannen's Taxi Service. "I want a taxi immediately, to take me to Mr. Ross's," she said.

"Not call at *all?*"

"Not call at all," John said. "We'll say we tried but the line was busy, and we couldn't pass the house without stopping in to say hello. He'll be forced to offer hospitality one way or the other."

They drove through the graceful little village center of Mute and then started the long climb up curving roads.

Theirs was the sixth car in a row now being parked in the Ross driveway.

"Impressionist painting, Mute style," John said, when before getting out of the car he observed the couples variously disposed. Eating strawberries and cream as they sat on the low wall of the stone terrace, standing with glasses in hand under the birches, or sitting on the grass, the whole scene bathed in swaying green light and deep sparkled shadow.

Marta emerged from the open front doorway with a trayful of food which she placed on the terrace table. Harley followed her with a bottle.

The uninvited guests advanced upon the terrace.

Elizabeth felt the shock in the man beside her as strongly as she felt her own.

Harley looked years older, with great dragged beagle pouches under his eyes. His tan had a greenish hue, and he seemed unreal, an immense drained doll, grinning, laughing, talking in his forceful voice but with the merriment gone from it. What had begun to look like a slight paunch had disappeared, but the flatness did not suggest hard, muscular strength.

He was pouring himself an immense drink when he saw them, a few feet away.

Elizabeth went over and gave him a light hug. "We were passing by, couldn't go on our way without saying hello, we tried to call you but the line was busy—" hearing the winded sounded in her voice.

"John, Elizabeth, what a nice surprise," Marta said. She moved to Harley's side. Fresh, solid, rosy, the green on her cheeks and columnar throat a radiant reflection of grass and trees, not the tint of awful illness. She wore a long crinkled white Mexican cotton dress ruffling over her bare feet, and had tucked an early rose, the palest pink, into her chignon.

(Later, John said, "She looks as if she's been feasting on something, or someone. Him?")

Meeting John's eye, over the glass from which he was thirstily gulping, Harley fell into an enormous spasm of coughing and choking. Recovering, panting, he said, "Stop looking at me like the head surgeon at Harkness Pavilion trying to decide whether I'll survive the knife, John." The old Harley flashing forth for a moment, reassuringly; and then the other, new Harley added peevishly, "I've been sick, fever, throwing up, couldn't keep a thing on my stomach, this is only my third day out of bed."

John hadn't foreseen the people, talking busily but listening, too. "May Elizabeth and I borrow you from your guests for a short time? We can't stay long."

"Why? Have you something of an interesting nature to disclose? Are you two getting married?"

"No," John said, not allowing himself the luxury of a glance at Elizabeth. "There are a few matters, your new English contract, for instance."

"Well, let us repair to the waterfall for our conference, but first get yourselves drinks, I'm not strong enough."

The Ingrams were sitting by the waterfall, but they were deep in the *Times* crossword puzzle. Harley elaborately collapsed into a white canvas director's chair and said, "Yes, the English contract? I thought that—"

That what? He was only making sounds to redirect John McIndoe's intent and reading gaze. Although in a way it was comforting to have John at hand; in spite of the ten years' difference in their ages, his agent was and always had been a strong home base. Not only in the business sense, although John was remarkably competent.

Talk, get away from the marble slab with the McIndoe microscope poised over it, studying the damage in all its horrible glaring colors. "I mean, I thought that you'd screwed the bastards *back—*" and then he was interrupted by Perdita Twinn, exploding around the corner of the house.

"Mr. Ross, Mr. *Ross* . . ." She wore her white going-to-church gloves and her blue straw hat was crooked. "The most awful thing, I felt I had to get to you right away, I've had this note—"

The pour of breathless words stopped for a minute, and then as if she could no longer bear the burden of private knowledge, listeners or not, "It says somebody wants to kill Mrs. Ross."

Even the waterfall seemed to hush itself, hang itself, make room for the words ringing through on the clear air.

Words that had nothing to do with the *Times* crossword puzzle, the glasses of gin and tonic in the tightening hands, the peace of May in sunny Mute.

Somebody wants to kill Mrs. Ross.

There was a strange sound from one of the Ingrams.

"It was just this morning," Perdita babbled. "I read it in church and I'm afraid I turned a little faint, and then I had to go home and rest, but I thought the sooner you knew the better. It said she'd come back to the wrong place at the wrong time. . . ."

Mildly appalled, Elizabeth looked at the thin fortyish woman in the incongruously crooked neat hat. She thought that in some way the woman was enjoying this, in spite of her evident distress.

John's eyes were on Harley and he apprehended a fleeting look of pleasure, or satisfaction, something accomplished, before Harley said:

"Good God, Perdita—let me see it." She took the folded paper from her handbag and watched anxiously as he read it.

"I don't suppose Jill—" He frowned. "Although perhaps with the left hand . . ."

TWELVE

Perdita Twinn's vaporings effectively scuttled the proposed English-contract conversation. Her raised voice, with its unlikely message, brought a fascinated audience around from the front of the house.

"Don't you think that that poor—that Miss Twinn should sit down?" asked Alison Hyde.

From the near kitchen window, Marta said, "I'm making her a cup of tea." She emerged in several minutes, bearing the cup. Perdita, the center of attention, began to weep, in anticlimax. "I am so sorry—in front of everybody—the second time today—I didn't mean—"

"Harley's always getting crank letters along with the nice ones," Marta said soothingly. "I hope you take sugar? It's unfortunate it had to be you this time."

Only too eager to have the darkness explained away, Perdita didn't pause to question the logic of this.

Mrs. Nairn was soundly napping above, but Dove, at the window, saw it all and heard every word, except when three or so people were talking at once.

Kill Mrs. Ross. The wrong place at the wrong time.

Something sent John's gaze upward. He saw the pale, child's face at the window and caught the look of naked fleeting terror on it. Instinctively, he made a beckoning gesture, arm lifted, forefinger angling back toward him.

She responded quickly. The slight thin figure in lilac gingham drifted out at the back door and skirted the group around Perdita.

John said in a strong overhearable voice to Elizabeth, "Who's

77

that little girl? She reminds me of my niece.''

This was interesting, as he had neither brother nor sister.
''Mrs. Nairn's niece, Dove, they call her.''

He went over and said, ''Hello, Dove,'' and introduced
himself to her. She looked up at him with a confidence and
trust—that came to her, oddly and immediately—in this tall
man whose eyes had sent to her a swift message of warmth,
of comfort. A stranger, she'd never seen him before. Dressed
in a nice thin rough-surfaced gray suit, a pale yellow shirt, a
dark gray wool tie. He didn't look at all like her father, except
maybe around the eyes, dark gray like his tie, but—

He bent and took her hand. ''Strawberries and cream going
begging on the terrace in front,'' he said. ''Would you care to
accompany me?''

She would indeed. She felt for the first time in a long while
lapped in safety.

He sensed that she was a child one could be direct with.
Spooning fruit for the two of them, he said, calm, casual,
''What's frightening you so, Dove? Was it just that woman in
the blue straw hat?''

''No, not just her.'' Telegraphically, eyes on his, Dove went
on, pouring it out, wanting to get rid of it, ''People being
expendable. The names he called her, the words he used, when
she came back. Arsenals—weapons, ammunition. Mr. Ross
crying, when he thought nobody could hear him. And saying
by God he wouldn't have it—'' She stopped to get breath.
''Aunt Em says married people do fight, but I don't know . . .''

As the look of woe came back to her face, John felt a faint
guilt, a trampling on some delicate shrinking place, along with
a coldness on his spine.

''Eat your strawberries, do,'' he said, setting her an example
by starting on his. ''I'm Mr. Ross's agent. Between us we'll
get everything straightened out.''

''Will you?'' The clear believing eyes disturbed him. He
said, feeling somehow that he was making a promise on which
his basic honor rested. ''Yes, one way or another, we will,
Dove. Now I must get back to my girl.''

''Who's your girl? Elizabeth? I saw you standing beside
her.''

"I think so," John said mystifyingly. "Do you like her?"

I . . . love you, Dove thought, but, gracefully, "Yes, she's nice. I'm going back upstairs, I'm not supposed to annoy people and get underfoot, and now I think I can read again."

"Best thing in the world, saves your soul or at least your sanity," he encouraged. "I'll see you before I go, Dove."

Rejoining Elizabeth, he felt a great interest in the elastic-band tension between them, reestablishing itself instantly. In a way this was as important to him as his concern with the Ross troubles.

He took her hand and led her to the edge of the pool. "Are you subject to gastric attacks or anything of that nature?"

"No," indignantly, "why?" But she thought she knew what was coming.

"We'll get nowhere with him in this social whirl. Would the advertising business grind to a halt if you took tomorrow off? Here?"

"For God's sake, John, I can't insinuate myself—"

"Please, Elizabeth, *please?*"

"Anything to save your income from dropping off—no, I take that back."

"You'd better." His hand, still holding hers, was crushingly hard for a moment. "And now do your stuff."

She went upstairs to the bathroom, stood considering, and then took a little case of eyeshadow patties out of her handbag. She rubbed lavender-blue lightly into the skin of her face and throat, removed the excess with a tissue, touched it up with a little more eyeshadow, pale green this time, and to the face in the mirror said, "Well, you do look ghastly."

Remembering where Mrs. Nairn's room was, she knocked at the door. Mrs. Nairn registered startled concern.

"It's nothing—this awful stomach of mine, maybe the strawberries? Is there somewhere I could lie down quietly, somewhere near a bathroom in case I— And will you explain to Mrs. Ross, and say not to bother to come up, I'm really not well enough to see anybody right now—"

She was cluckingly conducted to a blue-and-white bedroom.

It was trying enough to have John, at three, come in with ostentatious quietness and lay a palm on her forehead. "Poor girl," he said. "Yes, you'd better go back to sleep, you look frightful . . ." for the benefit of any anxious listener outside the door; and then depart on his hale and merry way to New York.

It was even more trying as hour followed hour to force herself to stay on the bed, a light summer blanket over her. There were tempting books on the bedside table but it wouldn't do to be discovered greedily reading one of them.

At seven by her watch, thirst and hunger drove her into action. She washed off her eyeshadow coloring, brushed her hair but omitted makeup, and went slowly and carefully down the stairs.

The living room was empty, the house silent. Then she heard, from the workroom, that human sudden noise, a sneeze. Her business here was Harley. Get on with it.

She found him studying the jacket of one of his books, the back of it, which showed a dramatic black-and-white photograph of him, close-up. He looked curiously like a man trying to make sure of his identity. "Hell, yes," he said. "There he is. So eager to talk to you, tell stories to you, you can almost hear his tongue falling over itself."

"Harley," Elizabeth said tentatively, and he jumped.

"Good God, the walking wounded—are you all right now? Could you use a drink? I could. You scared me."

"I think," she said fraily, "I might get down a little dry white wine. I'm still a bit wobbly. Where's Marta?"

"Right behind you," Marta said. "I was just tidying up the terrace." Watching you, checking you? Elizabeth's instinct inquired; listening unseen a little way along the hall to hear what Harley and his niece would be saying to each other.

"Let's go and drink," Harley said. "There's always drink, isn't there."

"But first—if you'll excuse us, Marta—I have a private problem, a family thing, I want to talk about with Harley, if you don't mind."

Harley gave her a raking wary look, like a large trapped animal. "For the time being, I'm afraid you're going to have to tell your troubles to Jesus, Elizabeth, I'm not up to anyone else's problems."

Door slammed hard in the face. Get the hell out of my business. Great idea, John. How would you have handled it? Grabbed Harley by the shoulders and shaken the truth out of him?

"It's been a bad day," Marta said in apology for her husband. "That Twinn woman with her note, and Harley's having to talk to a dim police sergeant about it—and then all those people, he's really not up to company yet but he insisted—"

Their eyes met. Some kind of message had been sent and received.

Stranded in Mute, Elizabeth was served a glass of wine, an invalid's dinner of clear soup and thin toast, and advised by Marta to go directly to bed. "Take the pink room, to the left of the landing. The bed's been just freshly made up. You still look terribly pale."

Feeling that gnawing hunger as well as a blank frustration in the face of hovering mysteries would keep her awake, she took two aspirins. Soon the waterfall sounds, blending with a rush of rain, took over and she tumbled into sleep.

A violent, fearsome awakening, hands at her throat, thumbs pressing in, a voice, as from an immense distance, muttering "Here's just a taste of it—"

The blackness was absolute, or was she, in fierce breathless pain, dying—?

A powerful and desperate heave sideways on the bed tore the hands from her neck. Before they could resume their work, she found the switch on the bedside lamp, hearing her own rasping half scream, half sob.

Harley backed away from the bed. The pupils of his eyes were black, enormous, almost obscuring the blue. His face was inflamed, grotesque. He looked like a savage caricature of himself, modeled in scarlet wax. His mouth was, ridiculously, hanging open. He was panting, his chest heaving under the gold dragons on his black silk robe.

In a flash of hysteria, she thought, Could this be Marta's room? Is this the way he always approaches the act of love?

He collapsed on the end of the bed, hands to his face, no longer an image of terror, of death.

"I had this dream," he said into his hands, "that someone was trying to kill me and I had to kill them back, I think I'm sleepwalking, or was—" Tears were pouring down his face. Shaking his head sharply—waking himself from the murderous dream?—he reached for a pack of cigarettes on the bedside table and lit one. Just barely managing it with the trembling of his fingers.

Totally unable to speak, hand to her throat, she met his eyes, wanting to look away. No one should see this.

"Elizabeth. Promise me. I'm in terrible shape, I'm half destroyed, this would be the end of me if— For your father's sake, if not for mine, for Charlie's . . . I've been having these awful dreams, I find myself in the kitchen sometimes, or out on the lawn . . ."

Big radiant Harley. Abject and broken, imploring. It was unbearable. The illness exposed, polluting the lovely big room in the quiet house in the country. The weight and density of some terrible secret intruded upon.

Was he sane?

And then a warm urge of the blood asserted itself, along with an overwhelming pity. A sad emotion, pity, she discovered for the first time in her life, and in some way a demeaning one, for both parties. I'm up here, safe; you're down there.

A Ross, she put an arm around his shoulders and said, "It's all right, nothing would have happened anyway, you'd have stopped, I'd have said no thank you, as I did— Yes, Harley. I promise."

Marta was not an intuitive woman or a nervous one, but she had thought it might be as well, on the whole, to put Elizabeth into the pink room for the night.

There was, across the dinner table, that dangerous blaze in Harley's eyes, as he passed her the little saucer of Dijon mustard. Just such a look as he had had when, upon hearing that his first wife, Adele, had remarried, and to an editor at Macmillan into the bargain, he had picked up a Waterford crystal decanter and smashed it in the kitchen sink.

She had decided, in her solid Franco-German way, not to take Twinn's note seriously. Perhaps that woman Jill, as Harley

had hinted. Trying with a flyswatter of printed paper to scare
her away.

Or perhaps Harley himself, words his weapons. Never his
fists, or any other sharp and killing thing.

How silly of him, if it was he, though, taking such chances.
Pick up the telephone, dial 322-8888.

"Hello, Alison."

As was her comfortable habit, she fell into a deep dreamless
sleep, and heard none of the distressing sounds from the pink
room.

That was close, Harley thought, going back to his room.
Although I think I only meant to frighten her. Not Elizabeth,
what the hell is she doing in Marta's room? Frighten the bitch
away. A bluff. I wouldn't have gone through with it.

It had seemed, downstairs, as he broodingly watching the
dying fire—"That's you, Harley, flickering out"—a basic
necessity. The only decent thing to do. The only fair thing.

Take warning, Marta. Know thine enemy.

That crack about his insisting on company— Like taking an
electric prod to an unruly steer.

As though she could say anything, do anything, without fear
of any reprisal.

Yes, kind to warn her of what she was asking for.

But for a terrifying second or so, the knowledge of how soft,
how vulnerable the flesh of the throat was, under his thumbs.

In any case, I will never, never again have so much as a
drop to drink after dinner.

Or not until—

Dove waited, rigid with fright, on the dark stairway. She
was dimity-nightgowned and barefooted, on her return trip from
unlatching one of the living-room screens to let Custard in out
of the rain. The faraway persistent meowing had finally reached
and waked her devoted ears.

She sensed rather than saw the large shape cross the landing,
open the door, close it again. Silence, now.

Except, from John McIndoe's girl's room, a low worrying
sound of stifled weeping.

* * *

It wouldn't be easy to lie to John. It wasn't principle that gave her pause, it was his X-ray shrewdness. She wouldn't be lying, though; merely withholding evidence. But still. Better to avoid a face-to-face encounter. And their aborted business was finished and done with.

She went out on Monday night with a man whose charm had strangely lessened. On Tuesday, she was conveniently tied up in meetings, then in a casting session for Braceways Foods' new commercial.

When he did catch her, his voice was crisply impatient. "For God's *sake,* Elizabeth, don't they have telephones in any of those places where you go about your business? This is the fifth—"

"I'm sorry, I've been rushed—and all I have for you is a big round zero. Harley wouldn't talk to me at all, more or less ordered me to go to hell and leave him alone."

"And an intelligent woman would spend—what?—the better part of twenty-four hours on the scene and make no observations whatever?"

"I left at ten," Elizabeth said. "I'm afraid all I can offer you is the fashionable phrase—a love-hate relationship." Watch it. She could swear she was looking right into his examining eyes.

"I'll get it out of you one way or another. Right now I happen to be rushed too, no point in our continuing this verbal tiptoeing."

Promise me, Elizabeth. I promise.

But she wished she hadn't had to give him another hard shove in the chest, backward.

Following his instincts, disturbed by the question mark she had left hanging in his head, he invented a reason for calling Harley. John Faunt was anxious to have lunch with him and discuss the progress on the new book with an eye to scheduling, would he be in town in the foreseeable future? Harley said there was no such thing as a foreseeable future and John sighed and then said:

"By the way, is that little girl, Dove, anywhere around? I

want to talk to her about a book she might be interested in.''

When Dove came on the line, he said, ''Your friend John McIndoe, Dove. Will you call me back collect, right away, on a phone where there's nobody to listen to you?'' and gave her his number. Yes, she said, she would, sounding surprised and happy.

And yes, operator, he would accept a collect long-distance call. He picked up the phone before his and Anny's secretary, Rosita, could answer it.

''That was fast. Was Elizabeth all right when she left? I'm worried about her, I haven't been able to reach her.''

''She was all right in the morning. In the night, she screamed, or sort of . . . part way a sobbing noise. I had to go let Custard in—my cat—it was late. It was dark. And then on the way back I heard her crying. He'd, Mr. Ross, gone back to his room.''

A short silence on her end; she hadn't heard very much, and it didn't make any sense at all anyway, his talking about dreams. She felt guilty about using up this nice man's money.

''And then?'' John asked gently.

''I thought she might be crying because she was still sick, and needed something— I knocked on her door and went in. We both went down to the kitchen and she fixed us hot milk. With brandy in it. For *her*,'' Dove made clear. ''And then she said thank you, she was fine, she'd be able to sleep now. She looked much better.''

''You're a helpful girl in every way,'' John said. ''I hope to see you soon, Dove. Perhaps you and Elizabeth and I can get up a picnic.''

To square his conscience, he sent her a complete set of Jane Austen, bound in hyacinth blue calf.

THIRTEEN

"I saw in the *Times* poor Jim Harwell toppled over dead, heart, right in the middle of a game of squash at the Racquet Club," Harley said. "Remember him, Marta? Vice president, Q and R, very big in frozen foods. Which reminds me—I haven't had it put into my will yet—I want to be cremated. Please make a mental note of that."

In the little garden room off the kitchen, Marta was occupied in arranging freshly cut tulips in a silver luster pitcher and a crystal bowl.

"Really, Harley, on a lovely May morning—"

"It can happen to anyone at any time. Which would you prefer for yourself? Cremation or just plain old six feet under, the best hardwood or maybe metal, something handsome in bronze—"

"I'll let you know when I decide."

He had wandered from the kitchen into the garden room and stood watching her, hands in his pockets. It was ten o'clock in the morning.

The impossible had happened, a little while back. His book had given a last expiring breath, lain down, and died. He knew other writers occasionally experienced this disaster, but it had never happened to him before.

It seemed a pack of nonsense, all 110 pages of it. He didn't know his characters any longer, what they'd say, what they'd do; they had faded and blurred, and hung distantly in the air, like ghosts. A short time ago they had been telling him what was happening to them, what was going to happen.

The unspeakable truth was that his book, which had been brimming, blazing, throbbing in its youth, *bored him*.

In his workroom, he had let out a little choked sound of despair.

He saw himself in the not far distant future running through his money—with her ardent help—and winding up broke. Or, Christ, having to go back to what he mentally termed the manure heap of the advertising business, the horrors of working *for* someone, taking orders *from* someone, after being the triumphant master of his own world.

But no, forget it no one would hire him at his age, at anything like the salary he'd need. He had been making ninety thousand when he departed from his agency. To say nothing of stock and profit-sharing emoluments.

In a way it was a curious relief to know that in advertising, too, he was completely washed up.

A phrase that had nothing to do with his story of *Cissie and ᴊaesar* kept floating through his head. ". . . a gallery of murderers . . ." Now, where had that come from? A possible title or something, announcing itself to him from his subconscious? Maybe "a child's garden of murderers" was better? No, a gallery of murderers.

Unable to bear the silent stare of the typewriter keyboard, he got up and went to the kitchen. He drank a glass of buttermilk to take the bitterness of too much desperately swallowed coffee out of his mouth—surely the coffee, surely just one more cigarette, would get his broken machinery started again—and then saw Marta busy with her flowers.

She gave the yellow and white tulips in the pitcher a gentle shake and they fell gracefully into place. She looked pointedly at her watch.

"Unlike you, wandering about at this hour."

He had to tell someone, even Marta. "I can't. I *can't*—the damned thing's dead as a doornail."

"Darling, you mustn't allow yourself moods and temperament, you never did before. Now do go back and concentrate, I'm sure everything will work out in no time."

By God, he wouldn't be chased—yes, that was the word, chased—back into that room, or at least not this morning. That room, which had been the happiest and most productive place he knew, where he was really only fully alive.

Alarming, the heavy pounding of his heart at the tolerant complacency, the bloody ignorance, of "everything will work out." And the implied directive that he'd better get cracking, if the Rosses were to continue to live as amply and comfortably as they were used to doing.

He felt again under his fingers the throat of the night before last. Only, the wrong throat. He turned sharply, walked across the kitchen, and went out and got into his car.

He began whistling Rachmaninoff's *Isle of the Dead,* saw his face in the driving mirror, and was horrified. His eyes seemed to be popping out of his head and the whites were raw red. He deliberately composed his features and kept them that way until he stopped the car in front of Jill's pink brick house. She never went to her shop on Tuesdays or Fridays.

He lifted the dolphin door knocker and let it fall with a crash. She might still be in bed. Well, so much the better.

Coffee cup in hand, she opened the door to him. She wore a thin silk bathrobe of turquoise blue and her hair was attractively wild, not brushed and tidied yet.

"Good morning, Harley," she said, and from the first syllable he didn't quite like the temperature of her voice. "What brings you this way? At this hour? I thought your mornings were hermetically sealed."

"What do you mean, what brings me this way?" He took the coffee cup out of her hand, set it on a table, and put his arms around her hard. Strong and slim as she was, she was meltingly warm and soft, naked, under the silk robe.

After a second's hesitation, she joined his kissing. Everything was going to be all right, then. In one niche of his life at least.

But suddenly she pulled back, turned, and reached for her coffee. "I just wanted," she said, "to see how you tasted, I'd almost forgotten."

He had been savoring, along with the brief healing delight in her, the sense of being back, safe, in his other home. The front door opened directly into the small living room, with its cushiony downy chairs and sofa. Jill was a great believer in comfort. It was all pale, ivory and beige and faint lemon, a stage for her vivid lion-haired looks. Yes, nice to be here, but there was something badly wrong—

Well, naturally. In her place he'd have raised holy hell, gone after the man with his fists and possibly her, too.

It was her not very well-banked fires that had attracted him at the start.

"Come back," he said, holding out his arms. "You can kick me in the shins, if you like, and you could tear a bit at my hair if I had any."

From cool and contained, Jill turned extremely hot.

"I'm not here for your use when you feel like it," she said furiously. "If and when that woman leaves we'll see if there's anything left for us."

His arms dropped to his sides. There must be words to say, to break through this, but he couldn't find them.

"I liked you better anyway when you were Harley Ross. Not whoever you are now, let out by her for a little while."

"You mean, like a dog?" Very quietly.

Again, she was a little frightened of him, but rage and the sense of rejection were the stronger emotions.

This immense worked-at prize slipping through her fingers. The Marta puzzle, about which he had been obviously lying to her. She heard in a sort of humming, ". . and nothing for Mrs. Gaynor." And felt freshly the stinging slap on her face, the first and the last, she swore, such punishment of her life.

She walked over to the door and flung it open. "And now please do go—whoever you are."

Harley went.

No woman had ever spoken to him as she had.

He had never been in a position to be spoken to like that, by anybody.

Get the car away from the front of the house or she might— she was capable of such gestures in her rages—have the police tow it away.

Following a pattern he hadn't known was in his head at all, he put the car in a parking lot farther up Main Street, walked several blocks, and pushed open the door of Meyer's Hardware Store.

The boy was standing, hands spread wide on the counter, slouched over what on closed upside-down examination appeared to be a motorcyclists' publication.

"Where's Meyer?" Harley demanded.

"Had to take his wife to the hospital." Dark eyes dropping furtively to the magazine again. Without looking at Harley, he managed, "Anything I can do for you?"

"How much do you make here, a week?"

"Sixty-five lousy dollars." He closed his magazine and stood up straighter.

"How would you like a job for twice that? It might only be for a month but of course by then you'd be in a higher bracket, naturally you could ask for equivalent pay." Careful. Don't pour it on. A twister, meeting an unaccountably handsome offer, considers first whether he's come across another twister.

The lizard eyes flickered over him. "What's the catch?"

"No catch. It's just that in a town this size I can't find anybody to do garden work."

"I don't know nothing about gardens."

"No problem. I'll direct you. Yes or no? I'm a busy man."

"You don't even know my name—"

"Ken Bliven, isn't it? Someone mentioned you, I forget who, said you were a smart kid."

Ken Bliven knew very well who his proposed employer was. On televison and everything, big-deal writer, obviously loaded.

"Why not?" was his method of accepting the job. "I'll fix the old bastard, walk out as soon as he gets back from the hospital. Tomorrow? What time?"

"Tomorrow at nine sharp. Number fifty—"

"Yeah, I know where you live. Okay," Ken Bliven said. "Whatever it is, I'll give it a whirl."

Harley drove next to Phelps' Nursery, where his arrival was later equated with that of Santa Claus. He bought a hundred young cypress trees, several hundred dollars' worth of rosebushes, twenty-five flats of geraniums, twenty-five more of ageratum, four hundred pounds of white pebbles, a fountain with an electric pump, and ten poplars. "This will do me for a start," he said, making out his check. "I must have the stuff by eight tomorrow morning.'' Wilson Phelps gave him a frost-safe planting schedule for his flowers.

He felt, suddenly, in roaring spirits. A line from a song of his early youth ran through his head, Jimmy Durante singing it. ''I pick myself up, dust myself off, and start all over again . . .''

A quick trip to the Unicorn Bookshop on Main Street. ''Yes, Mr. Ross, certainly, Mr. Ross, we have several really good ones on gardening, and a basic that you really *must* have, such a lovely hobby, and you might like to know your book's still selling like mad, when does the next one, *Her Grace* isn't it, come out? Oh, July? too thrilling.''

His martini tasted better than it had for—how long? Well over two weeks, he thought; he'd somehow lost count of time, it seemed to resemble forever. Before he mixed his second drink, he went into the kitchen and said to Mrs. Nairn, ''Have we any steak? I'd like a nice steak for lunch. With some broiled tomatoes.''

''We have indeed.'' This was surprising. This was cheering. His appetite, usually hearty, had fallen off terribly. It had crossed her mind that maybe he had discovered he had some awful, some final disease, and that was why Mrs. Ross had come back, to be with him until the end. That would in ways account for the unhappiness in the house, the sense of rage, of violence just held in by a hair. The human cry to the heavens: But why did this have to happen to *me?*

''Bring it into my workroom, will you?''

She found him pouring over books at his desk, garden books they looked to be. Probably doing research for his own book, he was always very careful about the authenticity of his backgrounds.

As the delicious scent of the steak floated to his nose he leaped up and took the tray from her. Reassuring sound, the clatter of knife and fork before she'd even gotten to the door. Well, thank the Lord, he's on some kind of upswing.

Greatly refreshed by his steak, and by the room-temperature Canadian ale he had poured to accompany it, Harley went immediately back to work. He was a quick study and by three o'clock had a near professional-looking garden plan laid out on a pad of graph paper he had brought for the purpose.

Marvelous feeling, to be deep in a project that could actually be completed. To hear the whirr of the mind working, the hands bringing it to life.

It would cost a lot, the garden, but it was worth it. Even if—

But even then, it wouldn't be a lost investment, it would add greatly to the value of his property.

Ken Bliven, roaring up the Ross drive on a borrowed motorcycle, was sorely tempted to announce himself at the front door. He was as good as anybody, wasn't he?

But the serene gray french-windowed house front gave him pause. Better play it straight and cool. From such a house—big, expensive, some people had all the luck—he had once abstracted a television set, a man's solid gold Swiss watch, and a tape recorder. The police never got anywhere with it; and he had turned the unsatisfactory but useful sum of a hundred and twenty-five dollars for the lot.

Mrs. Nairn answered his knock at the back door. She gazed in questioning disfavor at him, even though Harley had informed her of his new hired help. Jeans, turtle-neck cotton jersey, clean and respectable enough . . . but the secret, flickering presence of him, the black satin fall of hair over the narrow low forehead, the eyelids like heavy hoods over the dark eyes . . .

Be charitable, she reminded herself. Probably brought up in an unhappy house, the wary darting look learned in, perhaps, preparing for and escaping from the blows of a drunken father or mother. Like her brother-in-law's sister's kid, poor mite. Give the lad a chance.

"Had your coffee? You might swallow a quick cup and then I'll take you in to Mr. Ross."

Five minutes later Ken was studying, in Harley's workroom, the garden plan. "I've traced this from mine so we'll both have one," Harley said.

Christ, what a back-aching job, worse than building the pyramids. He'd dropped out of high school when he was a sophomore; the truant officer had looked the other way because he was a troublemaker and the school didn't want him back.

But he did remember, about the pyramids.

"It looks like it's going to be very pretty," he said.

Having breakfasted on Persian melon and creamed mushrooms on toast, Marta went in her leisurely barefooted fashion to discover what was going on at the back of the house.

Mountains of nursery stuff, roots balled in burlap, flats of flowers, enough for the gardens of Versailles, or almost— Harley, in a foremanlike stance, hands on hips, directing a sweating boy who had just picked up a cypress almost his size.

"I'll rent a dolly later today, yes, I think we must have a dolly." Loud and enthusiastic and, she realized, almost unrecognizable.

"Harley, what on earth?"

"I've been planning this for months," he explained, beaming at her. "A garden, up at the top of the bluff, the view's spectacular from there."

"But won't it be expensive?"

"Very. But now it will serve handsomely as an anniversary present. Early June, remember? Although I've mislaid the date."

"But your *book—?*"

"This will give me breathing space to clear my head. Then, as you put it, everything will work out in no time."

FOURTEEN

It was not Harley's way to keep his current excitements to himself, whether it was a spectacular win at poker or the plot for a new book. Among other people he called, to tell them about his garden, was Evangeline Morse, feature editor of *Portico* magazine.

"I have a scoop for you, Ev, you'll have *House and Garden* gnashing. I'm putting something together for Marta, an anniversary garden. Great idea, isn't it? I've never heard of one before. You can come up and do your before photographs and then do your after ones later. And you'll want interim shots, of course. We were intending to ask you up for a weekend anyway."

"We?" Evangeline asked, raising her eyebrows. She and Harley had had a brief pleasant affair three year back. She intended to leap at it, however. Famous name, wildly attractive man, and the garden thrown in for good measure, what a wonderful idea. She'd plan for at least four pages, two of them or maybe all of them in color.

" 'We?' Oh, you mean as compared to *us*. Our fond friendship never came to light," Harley assured her. "And magazine editors make a nice change in house guests."

"Then, the hell with Manhasset," Evangeline said. "I'll be there, I'll drive up."

She made a practice of knowing everybody, and was a dedicated name-dropper. "I just got a call from Harley Ross, oh yes, we're old friends, even though he absolutely slaughtered me in *Kingdom Come*. You've heard, haven't you, that he and his wife are back together after two years. He's going to do

94

the most wonderful thing to celebrate it. . . ."

Of course, magazine schedules being what they were, it would be months before the proposed feature appeared. But in the meantime there would be the photographers, the bustle, the local gossip, and inevitably a story in the Mute *Observer*.

A man who was building, at impressive expense, an anniversary garden for his wife would certainly not be thinking of— careful, find the right words—wanting to rid himself of her.

He considered calling John McIndoe, who also had a large circle of acquaintances, but thought that the announcement of his project might call forth a firm Scottish, "Very nice. What progress are you making on *Cissie and Caesar?*" Like a goddamned schoolmaster. But not all Scot, Irish somewhere, the word-cherishing part of him. He wanted, suddenly, to go to dark contemplative John as a burdened Catholic to the confessional.

Yes, much better not to talk to him about anything, now or in the near future.

". . . And guess what," Polly Ingram said to Alison Hyde "He's making an anniversary-present garden for her, up over the waterfall. There'll be murder done when Jill hears this."

Jill did hear, and her reaction was not immediately murderous. Harley, she thought, doesn't give a damn about gardens or gardening. And he sounded as if he meant it when he said he couldn't stand Marta.

She remembered his once having spent a great deal of time, effort, and money to have an elephant from a small traveling circus, with its keeper, parade slowly in broad daylight three times around the house of a friend who was very often in the process of recovering from a bad hangover.

Is this another ploy, game? Another elephant? What is Harley up to?

It was providential that his rival and friend, the novelist Duffy Glynn, on the telephone, called him away from his cypresses. But he would have found a way in any case, even if it hadn't fallen into his lap like this.

"My typing idiot has the gall to have a baby right in the middle of Chapter Thirteen, a suitable number when you think of it. Is that woman of yours any good?"

"Magnificent," Harley said indignantly, and then was quick to add, "As far as her work goes, that is."

"Someone said she'd gone off her nut in church and shouted she was going to kill you wife."

"She does have her lapses, but I think she's harmless. I learned in a roundabout way that before Marta and I closed the gap she had informed a friend or two that she and I might come to be man and wife." His actor's instinct fully functioning, he said this with amused complacency. "And so far Marta's intact."

"You don't think she'd fly into some kind of fit and burn or mutilate my manuscript?"

"No, I think she has room for only one passion. I'd more or less guarantee her, at the typewriter."

Typewriter. Words floating. Titles. A gallery of murderers . . .

Marta felt like a cat which, having had a good meal, is sunning itself silkily on a windowsill.

Things had taken an unexpected turn for the better. It was touching to see Harley, in his usual grand-gesture manner, trying to make up for his weeks of sturm and drang.

A long box of clothes from the Green Eyes Boutique in Westport had just arrived and was waiting to be unpacked.

From the kitchen came an aroma of split pea soup cooking, with a ham bone in it. She loved pea soup. And her house about her, shining, ordered, without her having to lift a finger.

Alison expected for lunch, although perhaps it was no longer necessary to keep bearing down on the Hydes. But she was good company anyway.

Her dentist's appointment behind her, for this week. Such a good man, Doctor Wingate, never a twinge. He turned out to be a devoted gardener and was much struck when she told him about the anniversary present.

"What a lovely thought," he said. "Rinse, please. A green

monument to a marriage. With the cypresses, giving pleasure at all seasons. You've supplied me with an idea for our anniversary. Not on that scale, but perhaps a rose arbor. Yes, a rose arbor. I wonder if we're too far north for Gloire de Dijon, I must look into it."

Even for a busy and well-paid woman, Elizabeth continued to be remarkably unavailable.

Sorry, she's on location. Greens Farms, Connecticut. Or working later at the Hammer Studios, couldn't take calls. In a meeting. In another meeting.

And did she never stay at home in the evenings?

Doesn't want to, doesn't dare, talk to me face to face, John concluded.

On Thursday, the evening pleasant and balmy—brisk exercise never hurt anybody—he walked up from Stuyvesant Square to her apartment building on East Seventy-third Street. He reached it at five-thirty and prudently entered the lobby so as not to be spotted lying in wait, as it were, under the canopy. The doorman remembered not only his face and name but his tips, and cordially spun the revolving door for him.

Luck or maybe a touch of ESP, there was Elizabeth, being spun in at five-forty, looking very fresh and fit for such a hard-working late-night woman, in a dashing raspberry red cape that danced and floated as she walked.

She stopped dead with a great forward swing of cape as he arose from his chair. She said brightly, "Well, good *eve*ning."

Perhaps he was waiting for someone else. There were eight hundred tenants in the building.

He reached for her hand, took it firmly, and joined it with his other hand.

"The Bell System hasn't been working for me," he said. "I walked all the way up from the square. The least you can do is offer me a drink. Before you take up your duties in Greens Farms or at the Hammer Studios, or perhaps you're expected back at the agency for another meeting."

She burst out laughing, a pleasant catching sound.

(Evangeline Morse's friend Alec Gorham was the current

man of a friend of her own in the next office up; and she was
now armed with innocent information to pass along to Harley's
agent.)

"I am going somewhere, but not for a little while, yes, do
come up." Skulking wouldn't have worked forever anyway,
not with this determined man. Be nice, be friendly. Old acquaintances sharing a drink.

The apartment was very much as he remembered it. Female
without ruffles or fluff, warm gay colors, a great bowl of
marguerites on the coffee table—flowers were one of her ex-
travagances—an open book face down on the arm of the sofa,
soft surfaces of velvet and taffeta and linen. She had added an
attractive bookcase which went up on both sides of the door
to the bedroom and across the door top.

She took off her cape, creamy suit under it, foulard scarf
tied high around her throat to conceal the now very faint bruises.

"Sit down while I get things."

"I always fixed the drinks," John said. "Remember?" He
gave her his long gray gaze. Remember was the wrong word
here in this room, with this man. Remember him as expert
bartender. Remember him one chilly morning looking delightful, ridiculous, in a yellow quilted calico robe of hers. Remember his laughter when she was once caught by a hiccup
in the middle of a kiss. Remember, deep in the night, with the
skies exploding overhead and lightning flaring through the cur-
tains, his arms reaching for her, pulling her to him, his murmured, "It's not a thunderstorm, it's just me."

Move, talk, cut the stillness. Old friends. She flicked on the
radio, thought she wouldn't go into the bedroom to hang up
her cape, said, "All right, make mine light, I must save my
strength for later on—"

Coming back with two frosty glasses, he said severely,
"You've got vodka instead of gin but I'll make do with it."

"A habit I caught from someone, I suppose," Elizabeth said
vaguely. She was on the end cushion of the sofa. He sat down
on the center one, perhaps a foot away from her.

He lifted his glass to her and said, "Elizabeth, why were
you—"

In a way that was unlike her, she interrupted him and took

the floor. "Good news about Harley, although slightly mad. But then, he is. Did you hear about his garden?"

"What garden?"

She told him about it, adding, "It's going to be photographed by *Portico*. Trust Harley to place his sentimental gesture before the public eye."

Briefly scowling, he said, "Damn it, his typewriter's his garden. I've never known him to take up such a fancy in the middle of a book before. And I've never known you to be gullible or softheaded, you haven't aged *that* much since our close association."

He got up and walked restlessly from one end of the room to the other. "It's not good news at all, something was badly wrong and now it's even wronger, maybe this elaborate affair will be centered with a mausoleum—"

The telephone at her elbow rang. She said into it, "I won't be fifteen minutes or twenty—just give me time to change."

"As I am to have only a few minutes," he said when she replaced the receiver, "what were you crying about, Elizabeth? Up there in Mute, in the middle of the night?"

In the sudden blank silence she picked up her drink and set it down again; she wasn't sure about her hand.

"I have a private life," she said in a voice that sounded faintly winded. "Underline private."

"That's no answer." He sat down beside her again and turned her to face him, hands on her shoulders. "Look me in the eye, Elizabeth. Why were you crying?"

"Who told you I was crying?"

"Dove."

"Have you been up there since—?"

"No. Telephone."

This was an excellent jumping-off point for righteous indignation, for getting a little security back. "I don't think you should use that child for your personal and financial reasons. You know Harley's temper. If he thought Our Man from McIndoe and Adams, Incorporated, was living in his house . . ."

In view of the arcane information about the garden and the ungoverned mental state it seemed to indicate, he thought she had a point.

"You're right and I won't," he said. His hands were still on her shoulders. "I'm sorry your private life is so sad. Is there anything I can do to brighten it up?" He kissed her, lightly and lingeringly at first, and then with force.

After a few moments, but gracefully, she released herself; she had gone her special pink.

"That was just to renew our friendship. Formally," he said, eyes inches from hers. "We are friends, Elizabeth?"

"Yes, of course—now I must run—"

"Run, then, run," tolerantly, rising to go. "But no matter how fast or how far, I will catch up with you."

FIFTEEN

"What's that rotten kid doing around here, Mr. Ross?"

Kenniston, the lawn man, had a powerful streak of what is known as Yankee independence. He sounded as if his own private property had been invaded.

"I believe in giving the young a helping hand. A pocket with some money in it is a deterrent to misbehavior," Harley said. "He's helping me put together a garden, a present for my wife. I thought of you of course, but as you grudgingly dole me out two afternoons a week and think you're doing me favor at that— And he's really putting his back into it."

Kenniston ignored this commendation. "Senator Hyde keeps me pretty busy," he said crisply. "Greenhouses and all. And the orchards. And not this convenient little piece of lawn, but the better part of an acre."

Ken Bliven had of necessity put his back into it part of the time; you didn't get trees and plants and pebbles dollied up a precipitous path without doing so. But, as was his nature, he rewarded himself for each long haul with a good lounge.

Harley had, to induce contented and continued work, carried up on the dolly a portable refrigerator which he kept stocked with his expensive Canadian ale. There was also Coco-Cola and ginger ale, but these innocent refreshments remained untouched.

Ken was sprawled in the warm sunlight, propped up on one elbow, drinking ale, when he heard a soft light step behind him.

It was Dove's first visit to the high airy garden. "Be nice to him, polite, but keep your distance from that boy," Mrs.

Nairn had counseled. And then so as not to sow undue fears in a young mind, "They're a bit wild sometimes at that age, I suppose it's only natural."

She had mislaid Custard, poor Custard so heavily close to having her kittens. Love and anxiety armed her, even though without any need of warning she wanted no part of the lizard boy.

". . . saw a strolling cat and aimed his motorcyle . . ." She had to remind herself that that was only on paper; Mr. Ross was reading it. And he wrote stories, not lives of real people.

"Have you seen my cat?" she asked politely. "She's pale yellow, almost white."

"Rubbed around my legs while I was trying to work yesterday," he said. "I felt like kicking her over the edge." He sensed her fear of him and found a tickling flattered pleasure in it. Pretty kid, hair almost as shiny as his own.

She winced visibly and her gray eyes rounded. "Please don't hurt her—she's going to have kittens."

"Who needs kittens?" He finished his ale in a long luxurious gulp and, thinking she might tell tales to that tough housekeeper aunt of hers, added, "No, I haven't seen it today and I got to get busy."

The wayward Custard was found ten minutes later and gently patted on the head. Mustn't pick her up, the kittens might fall out.

In the kitchen, she was silent for a time, watching her aunt at work at the counter. Then she said, "Can I get a collar and leash for Custard? Out of my allowance?"

Mrs. Nairn was deep in the intricacies of her salmon mousse with cucumber sauce. Mrs. Ross was having guests to lunch. Absentmindedly, she said, "May, not *can*, is the correct way to ask that question. And cats don't like collars and leashes—why?"

It was impossible to put it into words, to repeat it. It would make it real.

"I'm afraid she might get lost, or hurt."

"She's a home-loving animal and who'd hurt a cat? Get out the blender for me, Dove, for my sauce."

Ken didn't much care for the work, even with his ale and his extended rests. It was a sweat and a drag while he was actually at it. But the house and its tenants interested him. Money around. Mrs. Ross, pillowy-pink and golden-braided, looked like some lay. Maybe too old, though. She showed no interest in him, unlike that Mrs. Grainger whose husband had hired him for a week to build a dog run for his poodles.

It never hurt to get an angle on people, take a secret look into their lives, see what they were up to. Most people in his view were up to something.

Mrs. Nairn found him one noon, when he thought the house was empty, examining the contents of the green lacquer desk in the living room. He had his hand on the large checkbook to see what their bank balance was when from the doorway she said sharply, "Just what are you doing in here?"

"I was looking for a Kleenex, those geraniums make my head run," Ken said.

"I'll thank you to supply your own Kleenex out of your own salary, and speaking of salaries I'll thank you to get back to work."

On a rainy evening the next day, he saw a dim light in his employer's workroom and with an automatic slyness went to the window, standing at an angle where he couldn't be seen, and peered in.

The big body was face down on the leather sofa across the room. Was he drunk? Or crying, maybe? No, his shoulders were still. As he watched, the arm hanging over the edge of the sofa moved. The head turned toward him and a fingertip began to trace, over and over, the pattern of the blue rug, some kind of crazy rug with horses on it, and flowers and birds.

Was that the way people wrote books and made a lot of money? Was that how people looked and acted when they were *thinking?* Soft life, he thought, hand going to the muscle-pulled small of his back.

"Promise me you won't go up there until it begins to shape a little," Harley said, lunching on Monday with Marta and Polly Ingram. "Right now it's like the untidy dessert Winston Churchill handed back to the waiter at the Savoy. 'Take away this pudding, it has no theme.' ''

"Bob never planted so much as a daffodil for me," Polly
said. "Aren't you wonderful? And I can't ever remember having a weekday lunch with you before."

Harley's abandonment of his workroom and his work—he
had told her long ago he could never write in his head, away
from his typewriter—disturbed placid Marta. It was as though
the gas or electricity had been suddenly shut off; some essential
amenity threatened.

But she preened a little for Polly's benefit. "I'll hold off as
long as I can stand it. But I'm only human, darling."

She held off until three o'clock that afternoon, when Harley
drove away to get, he said, four gardenias in tubs. And came
upon Ken Bliven, fast asleep in the sunny long grass, with an
empty ale bottle in his hand and another beside him.

She saved him for a bit later and examined the work done
so far. The cypresses, she saw, were to be set in a circle and
the garden laid out within the circle. An ambitious project,
about sixty feet in diameter, she calculated. There had been
great secrecy about the plan when that nice Evangeline Morse,
with her photographer, had arrived for the weekend. "Go away,
Marta, and play, while Ev and I get down to business."

With one sandaled foot, she gave a light kick at the sleeping
boy's leg. He woke to see her, sunlit and looming, and his
first dazed furious thought was *Who the hell do you think you're
kicking?*

"Do you do this all day, up here, or just part of the time?"
Marta asked in the brisk tone of authority.

He scrambled to his feet. He still had the bottle in his hand;
he looked at it and then dropped it to the grass. "It's hot work,"
he said.

"Well, but you're being paid for it, aren't you?" She must
remember to ask Harley how much. "I'll just sit on this nice
rock and see what a good gardener you are, shall I?"

Raging under the blue gaze—she was his grandmother, his
high school principal, the chief of police, all the detestable
finger shakers and commanders—he spaded out a deep hole,
half filled it with water from a ten-gallon drum, and planted
his sixteenth cypress.

What if she comes up here every day to spy on me? What if she finds me asleep again? And kicks me? One way or another, I'll fix her, he thought.

He started another hole, not even wanting to look at her, but after a dozen spadefuls or so felt a silence, a vacuum. She was gone. He went and opened another ale. The rest of the hole could wait while he drank it.

"How much are you paying that boy to lie around sleeping—in a sea of ale bottles—when he's out of your sight?"

At the dinner table, Marta asked this silkily as she began on her lobster thermidor.

"I told you to stay away from there!" Harley was instantly furious. "That's my territory for a while, until it's finished. Has the lady of the manor been scolding him?"

"No, just woke him up."

Couldn't she keep her hands, her trampling bare feet, out of any inch of his life? Push back the rage—

"Fifty dollars a week. To me he's just a strong back, two arms, two legs. You can't be choosy these days. So for God's sake don't rock my boat."

Too bad it had to be another rainy day.

Lightly skimming a few final globules of fat from the surface of her fragrant vegetable soup, Mrs. Nairn said to Dove in a letting-down-lightly manner, "I've had this note from your father. He won't be here now until July, something about a convention he has to go to. He'll be writing to you later in the week, he says, but he wanted me to break it to you."

Dove tightened her swiftly closed eyelids against tears; a habit that without being aware of she had picked up in the last month.

Hastily Mrs. Nairn said, "Soup's all taken care of. I think for our own dessert tonight we'll have cut-up oranges and bananas and coconut, we both like that. It'll be July before you know it."

Feeling strangely bereft, in the scented kitchen filled with waterfall sounds, Dove said, "I think I'll go and read one of my new books."

"Good, but no tears, dear."

Dove went up to her room. She opened her pretty blue *Northanger Abbey* and heard again the voice, not like her father's, but— "Strawberries and cream going begging in front . . ."

She went to her small white desk and found the New York number he had given her, scribbled on the blotter. She transferred it to the inside of one of the butterfly-shaped notes her father had sent her for her birthday. Her spelling was excellent, but she had never seen his name, only heard it. The closest she could get was Mr. Mackandough. Where to put it? Under her pillow. Just for luck. And comfort and company.

Perdita Twinn's timid voice on the telephone, shortly after the once sacred hour of two: "Would you have any objection if I worked on Mr. Glynn's manuscript, Mr. Ross? I wouldn't like you to think—but then, it will be some time I suppose before you're ready for me—"

"Perfectly all right. In fact, I recommended you highly to him."

Happily, warmly, she said, "Thank you so much." And then, timid again, "Was there anything more about that awful note?"

"No. The police have it, I suppose they made a routine check of the town cranks. But as Mrs. Ross told you, nasty mail is occasionally showered on my head."

She had given him an idea. Leave no stone unturned; this was a stone that wanted attention. He must remember to think consistently; now, of all times, to follow things up. Until now, he'd just been going along, minute to minute, impulse to impulse. But that wouldn't do from here on in. Too dangerous.

He got out his anonymous Woolworth scratch pad and spent ten minutes laboriously printing with his left hand. This task finished, he went upstairs and got his pigskin gloves from his dresser drawer, put the notes in the cheap plain envelopes he used for paying bills, and stamped them.

Fifteen minutes later, they went into the Local Mail slot at the Mute post office.

At two-thirty the following day he picked up the telephone

and dialed the police station. Upon giving his name, he was instantly and respectfully switched to Chief Bello. Mr. Ross always gave generously to the annual police picnic for the underprivileged children of Mute (there were about twenty-five of them) and, besides, he was famous.

"Sorry to trouble you, Chief," Harley said, "but I've gotten this peculiar note. Let me read it to you. 'Somebody's out to get you and I mean but good. As they say you're an atheist, I guess you won't have to bother about saying your prayers, but just as a clue it will be when you least expect it.' You'll remember my wife got one several weeks ago, same paper, same printing, at least to this amateur eye."

"Good God almighty," Chief Bello said. "You're the third one today, Mr. Ross. Sid Meyer got one—nothing about atheist in it of course—and so did the manager of the phone company, Mr. Bricker. We got nowhere with your wife's note and while the file's still open we kind of thought—"

"Yes, I know. Probably ordinary everyday nuttiness. I'm still inclined to think so too." His choices had been good; nobody could possibly suspect Meyer of having some sinister secret buried in his past, revenge finally about to be taken; nobody could possibly fancy any dark tie between Harley Ross and the manager of the telephone company. "I just notified you because I did wonder about the other people in town being pestered in this way."

Thinking of the picnic, August not all that distant, Bello said, "I'll stop by and pick it up myself, check for fingerprints, although your wife's note was clean."

"Good. A crank, nine chances out of ten, funny how they develop in the pure healthy air of little towns. But you never know, do you?"

SIXTEEN

.

"What in heaven's name has come over Harley?" asked Harley's publisher John Faunt of John McIndoe. "I've heard he's stopped all work and is constructing a maze or some such thing."

John gave him a brief gloomy resume of the little he knew or surmised about what had come over Harley. It was a relief to complain to a financially sympathetic ear.

"—and on the strength of the first four chapters I've got Janeway Films in a lather to buy it. I sketched the rest of the plot for them, the hard way—I made most of it up. They're talking about Elizabeth Taylor for Cissie. God," added John into the phone, "I could kill myself."

"I'll be going on up to Lenox for the weekend. Do you think it would help if I stopped by with a little benevolent scolding and encouragement? In ways Harley's like a child, though a very large-sized one."

"You can try." Then inspiration seized John. "I have a much better idea. His work lapse seems to be more or less on cue with Marta's reappearance. If I were you I'd sweep her away to Lenox for a nice long weekend. She's not uninterested in names. You might . . ."

His point was quickly taken. "I think I can get Sergius to tear himself away from his troubles for a few days." The Secretary of State was John Faunt's brother-in-law. "And Kitty Riddle. That ought to do." Katherine Riddle was a grande dame of the Broadway stage.

"That ought to do nicely," John said.

"I don't suppose, dear boy, you'd care to join us? Angela,

as you know, has an unholy passion for you."

"No, thank you anyway. I have other Ross business to pursue this weekend, I think."

Harley could scarcely believe his eyes when the chauffeur-driven Bentley, with the Faunts and Marta inside it, disappeared around a curve in the drive.

He felt as he had at ten or eleven years old, on the first intoxicating timeless days when school was over for the summer.

John Faunt hadn't scolded; instead had, over his sherry, said, "Congratulations. Young John tells me your new book is all but on film."

John McIndoe had called him about that the day before. At the time, it had appeared to him as a fist shaken in his face. *Get on with it. Get on with what?*

Now, the prospect of freedom filled him with a heavy glow. A film . . . he'd never missed, from the first book on. Maybe, after all—maybe in sweet peace he could apply artificial resuscitation and bring the thing back to heart-beating romping life.

For the fullest use and enjoyment of this unexpected blessing, Marta's departure, he urged upon Mrs. Nairn a three-day holiday, starting immediately. She took no offense; with an openness that touched her, he said, "This is the best chance I've had to work in weeks and weeks. How about a whirl in New York, for you and Dove? It would all be on me."

"I don't fancy the trip, but I'd enjoy a spell with my sister-in-law. Thanks anyway." A no-nonsense woman, she and Dove had, within the half hour, departed.

"But he looks so *different,*" Dove said. "So . . . all shiny from the inside out."

Maybe this was deliverance. Maybe this was the sunlit waking end of a bad dream. The madman's garden up on the bluff. That, as Kenniston had so succinctly put it, rotten kid. Those lunatic notes.

It was three o'clock and his house was unbelievably and superbly empty. Nothing to hear but the waterfall and the stirring of the brains in his head.

He wanted to shout and sing but he said out loud, "Let your typewriter do the shouting, man."

No more alcohol; he made a pot of strong coffee and carried it in to his hot plate. Deliberately, he thought himself backward in time. How had he been feeling, what had he been thinking, before the near fatal knock on the door at twenty-seven minutes after eleven on that April morning?

Half hypnotized, he inserted fresh paper, poised his hands over the keys, and felt his fingers pulled as if by magnets. A paragraph. Another. A pour of dialogue, rough, but good. Smooth it later. Don't stop now, *don't stop—*

Two pages, three, four, or was it five? Yes, five. Stopping for a few seconds to pour coffee, atheist Harley said, "Thank God thank God thank God—"

In his empty, typewriter-clattering house, a voice said from the doorway, "Hello, Harley."

Without even turning his head, he said, "For Christ's sake go away."

"I'm not Marta, you know."

Now he did turn his head and gave her a brilliant, savage, triumphant grin.

"I said, go away. Whoever you are."

"No, Harley love, I won't. I'm told that Marta is off to Massachusetts to pass along her good counsel to the Secretary of State. It couldn't be a more ideal time for us to have a little visit."

Jill was, in her pink brick house, a thunderstorm that broke, retreated, circled distantly, and came back and broke again.

Not that you would know it to look at her, and she made sure, partying and entertaining, that plenty of people could see the handsome woman, so lazily sure of herself, so unaffected by the sudden rent in her life.

But it was, she thought, like being, without consent or even consultation, divorced at the start of a strong and happy marriage.

Her public calm stoked the fires of her private fury. Rejected. Kicked out. With only a thin skein of obvious lies to explain why. Marta enthroned in the gray stone house, looking as though she lived on cream. She had come into the Brookfield Center shop one day and asked if there was any Coalport china to be had. "Daisy," Jill called to her partner, "can you take

care of this customer?'' and loathing herself went into the back
office to telephone friends for cocktails. She was not a woman
given to retreat or inclined to patience.

A chance meeting with Bob Ingram at the French bakery,
on Saturday morning, dropped opportunity into her lap. They
both bought croissants for Sunday breakfast, then gossiped for
a few minutes.

She waited until the afternoon, and then drove to Harley's
house. Not *their* house, Harley's.

"It couldn't be a worse time, for me," Harley said. "I've
turned myself on at last. Please, darling Jill, absent yourself.
We'll have a party for two sometime—well, I don't know,
perhaps ten or eleven tonight."

"No. Now." Tight syllables flung at him.

Calm her down, get her out of here.

"I can give you fifteen minutes."

"Yes, I heard the typewriter, through the window, going
lickety-split. I've been told by friends you're allowed to see
that your book seems to be getting short shrift. Which shows
the sooner you get rid of that woman the better. That's why
I'm here."

"Clarify your point," Harley said. He got up and went past
her and into the living room. He didn't want the life-giving air
and atmosphere of his workroom to be soiled with weary re-
criminations. The air in here didn't matter.

Jill settled herself on the sofa, in Marta's corner, and patted
the cushion beside her. Not accepting the invitation, he leaned
with one elbow on the mantel.

She was wearing his tangerine shirt again, and her whipcord
pants. She looked dangerously glowing.

"I've sat still and taken it long enough," she said. "I have
come, not to ask, but to demand, that you end this nonsensical
reunion. I'll give you one week."

Harley was mentally back at his typewriter in the middle of
a paragraph. There was an invitation card on the mantelpiece.
He seized it and scribbled a few key phrases so he wouldn't
lose them.

He only half heard and half comprehended Jill's communique
from her battlefront.

What madness was this? Had she been drinking? Still with only a part of his mind and attention on tap, he realized that he didn't care what she felt or said, or why. Since that morning in the brick house when she had denied him his identity and ground her heel on his masculinity he hadn't cared at all.

"If you want to call it blackmail, call it that, okay. *She's* living on blackmail terms with you."

This reached him and hit him across the heart with the impact of a physical blow. "What the hell are you talking about? I have no contract with you that I know of."

"I don't just think, I *know* I was right, that very first day, when I said that bitch had something on you. What awful thing does she know about you that no one else knows?"

The silence in the room was profound. A light wind lifted the white lawn curtain behind Jill's head, wrapping her lion hair like a coif. Sun and shadow sifted through an aspen outside the window quivered over Harley's tall, motionless body. She wasn't afraid of him this time; her rage was her armor.

He hoped the giveaway veins at his temples weren't showing. His head felt as though it was going to burst.

"A drink might calm you down and restore at least some of your sanity," he said. He had to move, escape her eyes.

"Pour away. *You* probably need one. But I mean exactly what I say, Harley. If you don't get up off the floor and deal with her—one week—I'm going to do some digging. Start asking questions."

She touched one finger of her left hand with the forefinger of her right. "It would have had to have happened before she left you, that was two years ago."

She went on to the next finger. "Of course, it may be nothing really ghastly, just something the great man's ego wouldn't want known to his public. But it's *there.*"

His back to her, he poured two scotches. "I forget—do you or don't you take ice?" Was that his voice?

"What a short memory. Never. But thinking back, you do, don't you? I'll wait while you get it."

In the kitchen he wanted to run, run out the back door, run until he was spent and then fall on the ground and stay there.

"Thank you, Harley," accepting her glass. "I'll start by going through old newspaper files at the *Observer,* beginning with the year before she left. Something that happened, something that nobody had any immediate reason to connect with you . . . something that might ruin your professional life if it ever emerged. And it could very possibly have happened right here in Mute, you're a home-loving man. . . .''

Harley's mental computer, its programming in shock, produced:

But even if you win you lose, Jill. You can't get a man with a gun, as Irving Berlin wrote in that musical. I rose for a little while from the dead, there in the workroom. I got myself back, in spades. I can live with Marta and her twin sister if she had one, working again, functioning. By God, it was like downing a bucket of champagne . . . I think, but I'm already forgetting how it felt. You are about to send me back to hell and damnation. You are about to murder me. Hell hath no fury like a woman scorned. Yes, hell has. The fury of a man who was dead, and waked, and tasted his leaping strength again, and was given back to himself whole. Future blood wiped off his hands, sanity and peace back inside his skull. . . . I had this dream that someone was trying to kill me and I had to kill them back. Promise me, Elizabeth. The death of a child, hmmm, and not just any child, but Lavinia Hyde, hit-and-run driver never found. Let's see, here's the date, I wonder what Harley was up to that evening, I know all of his friends now, I can ask around. But this is to accredit her with the gifts of a seer, a witch. But it could happen, she might stumble on it. She was a piercingly intelligent woman. *To kill them back* . . .

All this, in the time required to reach for and light a cigarette and pick up and taste his drink.

Give her one last chance.

"What do you hope to gain? If you did find I'd cribbed a plot from somebody's book, or something—put a collar around a lover's neck? Take Marta's place, or what you think is her place?"

"This is the worst and hardest slap I've ever gotten. I can't go through life with it, wondering what happened to you and me. I plainly and simply can't live with it.''

It didn't matter what he said now; or only for a little while.

He forced himself to sit beside her on the sofa and gave every appearance of a man thinking desperately hard, his head hanging, his eyes roving the rug.

Finally, reluctantly, he said, "A week's not enough, Jill, give me two. I've been trying to get together a sum of money to speed her on her way. Pusillanimous of me but it's worth it, just her being here has pretty well shot my book down. Yes, you can call it blackmail but I don't care if I can get myself—if I can get you and me and a normal life back. I own part of a condominium in New York and I think I have a buyer. But I will need the extra time."

Her victory astonished her. Don't ask any more questions now, don't try to fill in any gaps. She'd find out all about it in good time. Ride this creaming wave.

She held out her arms to him.

"Harley, darling. It's been too long."

It was delicious to make free of what she now allowed herself to refer to mentally as Marta's house. To have a lazy late-afternoon bath. To say to Harley, "Go back to work, darling, now that it's going well. I'll just stretch out on the sofa and read. Whenever you're thirsty, let me know."

To share late cocktails, broil steaks for the two of them, with her Béarnaise sauce. But, "I can't eat," Harley said. "I suppose I'm too excited. About the book, and you."

Jill laughed. "I imagine it will always be in that order. Oh, well. I'll finish your steak for you."

To make coffee, and pour brandy into it, and then kindly urge more brandy, straight this time, upon Harley; his color was bad. But soon he'd be himself again, lusty laughing Harley, all his cylinders ticking over.

Late as it was getting, he seemed reluctant to go to bed.

"All right, I'm sleepy, I'll go on up now, wake me if I don't snap to attention the second you come in. . . ."

At ten minutes before twelve, using a ruby-red silk twill tie, hands shrinking and heart crashing, he ineptly but successfully strangled her to death.

SEVENTEEN

Feeling absolutely nothing, but aware of the tears pouring down his face, and brushing them impatiently away, he went ahead with the process he had planned in his workroom before cocktails.

He picked her up and carried her with some difficulty down the stairs and out the kitchen door, beside which he had placed the dolly. All this was done in darkness, but the house was not, in any case, in view of any other house at the back. He roped her to the dolly and began the trip through the orchard and up the path. A heavy weight to pull, but some surge of power placed itself at his disposal. It was a starry night, and his feet knew every step of the way.

Around the edges of Marta's garden, then another long climb, shallower this time, above it. Across a tilted meadow, into the woods. His property ran another acre or so, beyond them. His walks often took him through his woods. He knew the exact place. A soft small clearing, deep in brown needles, in the heart of the pine grove.

He found it, laid the dolly on its back, took the spade off it, and set to work. Deep, it had better be; well worth the back-breaking labor.

The night was cool, with a light wind, but he sweated heavily, his shirt sticking to him. It was a good two hours before he was satisfied with his grave, and another half hour before he had it filled in. His eyes accustomed to the night light, he tossed spadefuls of pine needles over the fresh earth. He was tempted to add armfuls of brambles on top, but no point in marking it in any way; he could touch it up in daylight with more pine needles if more were needed.

He went back down with the dolly, put it in its usual place, leaning against the garage, and went into the house. He put on one low light in the hall, took her handbag off the hall table, and removed her scarlet morocco wallet from it. He had thought of a use for the wallet, if it was ever required, which was unlikely.

The handbag he disposed of in the waterfall pool, weighted with stones. The current would carry it into the deep stream which ran well under the house.

Now the chancy part: her car. But not too chancy; close to four, his watch told him. Hands gloved, he drove it along the silent roads and left it in front of the house, where she always kept it. Main Street had hours ago gone thoroughly to sleep; the powers that controlled Mute allowed no bars on the carefully preserved, graceful street, with its shops and stores set in old, fine, colorful houses.

Using back roads, he walked rapidly home. Whenever a car's headlights showed in the distance, he concealed himself, behind a tree, then a board fence. There were only two cars, and one proceeded lurchingly as if the driver was so drunk he wouldn't know his own mother.

The scotch bottle tempted him, but once he started he might not be able to stop. Take two of Marta's sleeping pills instead. He'd want his wits about him. They'd served him well so far.

Pills taken, chemicals about to lead him into sleep, or to at least some sort of unconsciousness, he found himself thinking in a distant tattered way, gallery of murderers lessened by one. But he remembered what his mother used to say, when contemplating a hazardous family decision or action. Needs must when the devil drives.

In Jill's house, the telephone began ringing, downstairs in the living room, upstairs beside the bed. It was eleven o'clock on a sunny Sunday morning.

Either the passing of time or the vibration in the air caused a vase of anemones, white, powdery blue, and velvet red, to shed several petals, softly and slowly, on the glass and steel coffee table.

The screened windows facing Main Street were halfway open. Church-going traffic noises came sedately in. The handsome tiger cat from next door jumped hopefully onto the outer sill and peered in. Jill, perhaps in recognition of a certain likeness between them, sometimes gave the cat a bit of her late, lazy Sunday breakfast, a nibble of chicken livers or imported English bacon.

The telephone stopped ringing.

"Probably still in the sack," Joe Grundy said. "Telephone turned off or she just said, the hell with it."

"Try her in half an hour," his companion Mirabelle said. "She could be in the tub. *I* wouldn't get out of the tub if the Pope of Rome called."

"Limes do make all the difference in bloody marys," Polly Ingram complimented Joe Grundy. "I thought we might find Harley here, since he's all alone this weekend."

"Is he? I'll call him. I did try to get Jill, lucky in a way there was no answer. I wouldn't like to be accused of arranging assignations behind Marta's back."

Polly dimpled. "People nowadays can arrange their own assignations. I wonder . . . Jill not answering her telephone."

"Just for sport, let's just see, come with me while I call him."

Harley answered after ten persistent rings.

"I was outside counting geraniums to see if I have enough."

"Come on over for a drink?"

"I can't. Jill's on her way, she's going to stop off before she heads for New York with somebody or other." Man to man, he added, "Two loves have I. Awkward at times . . . but I'm sure you've been through it."

"Yes," Joe Grundy said sympathetically, "and something tells me I'm about to start it again. Well, happy geraniums, Harley."

Pursue, John said to himself, had been the correct word in reference to his other Ross business over the weekend.

He finally got an answer on the telephone at noon on Sunday. "Well, you are a butterfly," he said. "Or do you work weekends too? I thing your devotion to work is wonderful."

She smiled with pleasure at the burr of the resonant voice over the wire.

"I had to wash my hair," she explained. "You have to take a breather sometimes, for necessary chores like that."

"Is it dry yet?"

"Why? Are you trying to arrange another Harley conference? If so, I gather you work weekends too."

"Elizabeth," he said severely, "stop that nonsense. It's dangerously close to flirting. Is your afternoon free by any chance?"

"Yes, until six or so."

"You probably need fresh air and exercise after all your carousing. I'll walk from here and you walk from there, and I'll meet you on the terrace at the zoo at one."

"Why the zoo?"

"Have you forgotten that I like zoos? And anyway, why *not* the zoo?"

In the May sunshine, on the terrace in front of the cafeteria, they ate virtuous light salads and drank a bottle of beer each. The sun bestowed blue and amber flickers on her immaculate shining hair. Of necessity fresh and well rested, because he hadn't wanted anyone else's company last night when she proved unavailable, John in his Norfolk-jacketed Donegal tweed attracted interested looks from other lunchers, female.

For a while he thought he was going to get nothing out of Elizabeth but a delightful afternoon. They inspected the animals in a leisurely fashion, catching a young lion with his rump in the air and his front paws extended, like a playful dog. They studied the ancient, Hebraic profile of a Bactrian camel, laughed at an ape who conceived an instant dislike for and rage at Elizabeth and tried to rattle the bars of his cage at her. "But let's get out of the monkey house fast," she said. "You never know what frightful thing they'll be up to next."

From a caratina, John bought his first bag of roasted peanuts in their shells in years, and shared them with her. On the broad pathway under an arched bridge, he reached companionably for her hand and said, "Is your spare time—not that there is any—spoken for by one? Or many?"

"A few."

"To hell with ambiguities. I'll fix you." On the other side of the bridge was a large sycamore tree; they had left most of the Sunday strollers behind them. He drew her behind the tree and kissed her, not just an embrace but a basic personal message swiftly and strongly delivered.

He looked down at her expression of astonished recognition. "Haven't you figured this out for yourself? *Yet?*"

"Or do you mean, yet *again?*"

"I think I mean yet, still."

Not far away, a lion, perhaps the romping one, roared.

"One of the last times I remember, you were a thunderstorm," she said a little shakily, "and now you have a lion backing you up."

At six o'clock in the Birdcage Bar at the Carlyle—she had ruthlessly canceled an evening she hadn't much wanted anyway—she said slowly, "I made a promise and now I'm going to break it. I haven't any idea why I didn't know I could trust you."

"Today is more about us than about Harley," he said. "But I don't like the gap, and I keep hearing you crying. . . . When now or ever you tell me anything, you're handing it over to absolute silence."

She had a gift of total recall and with deep relief unburdened herself, word for word, moment by moment, watching him go from concerned to appalled.

When she had fallen silent, staring at her untasted drink, he said as if to himself, "If you're right about his thinking you were Marta . . . I suppose there's no way on earth to stop a man from killing his wife if he's set his mind to it. But one way or another it's his own sure death he's planning too. I must—"

"You must what?"

"I don't know," he said.

The grave, in deep shadow under the pines, was unnoticeable. But he scooped up forty double handfuls of pine needles and scattered them, to make it even more invisible.

He had been ready for Joe Grundy with his casual Jill-New York reference. Inevitably, someone would take pity on the weekend bachelor. Mike Heard took pity at three. Harley was waked from a numb heavy sleep on the living-room sofa and for a moment didn't know who or where he was, or whether it was day or night. Still dazed, blurred, he answered the telephone and said thanks, but he was working.

He had decided in the early morning that he wouldn't attempt work today. After all, he said, I have had very little sleep. And if it turned out that he couldn't—

But that was what it had been all about. His work, and women trying to destroy it, and with it destroy him.

No, let it go until tomorrow, when he'd be rested and able to look forward to another long day. All by himself.

Marta called him at five. Checking, he thought, to see if I'm here and alone, but how would she know if I was answering from a nice warm bed with a companion beside me?

"Yes, I'm fine, are you having a good time?" It was hard to hold in the sweep of red rage. *You* are responsible for the death of Jill, it wouldn't have had to happen if you hadn't come back.

"You sound odd," Marta said.

"It's that May allergy I have, the green tree dust or pollen or whatever it is in the air, I've been sneezing my head off."

Following a compulsion which had been growing stronger all afternoon, he drove, when dark had fallen, to Jill's house. Dreadful possibilities had presented themselves. She might have started a letter to him, a note, and then decided to come in person; he could all but see the note on her writing table. "Dear Harley, I'm afraid I'm going to have to give you an ultimatum . . ." She might keep a diary. She might have invited people for late Sunday supper.

He went through the brick archway into the small side garden and used his own key to open the garden door. No problem if someone spotted him. All Mute must know of the recent commitment of Harley Ross and Jill Gaynor.

There might be someone just passing, outside the front door.

He switched on the nearest lamp.

"Jill," he called up the stairway. *"Jill?"* This maneuver, and the echoes of his own voice, frightened him badly.

No note, no letter on the writing desk. No sign of a diary in the desk drawers, in any of the bookcases, or in her bedroom. A decoratively untidy woman—Roman-striped robe tossed over a chair, yellow sandals kicked off in the middle of the rug, a long amber necklace looped over the bathroom doorknob, a damp pink towel trailing from the edge of the tub in the still scented bathroom.

A quick glance into the kitchen. Reasonably in order, for her; dishes done but not put away. Nothing to suggest to the officially examining eye a depature unplanned-for.

The telephone rang and continued to do so for what seemed an interminable time. Naturally, she wouldn't answer it. She had gone off to New York.

Trying, over a nightcap and after midnight, to concentrate on the crucial final chapters of a manuscript, John put it down. Not fair to the writer, who had sweated his way through this.

Back to subject number one.

Call Marta and tell her to get out of the house, skip, because otherwise her husband might take it into his head to kill her?

Monstrous. Impossible.

Alert Mrs. Nairn? A woman of obvious common sense, tough and reliable. But was she to stand guard on them twenty-four hours a day? She might take fright, for Dove, and flee. Leaving just the two of them there.

The Mute police . . .? "As Mrs. Ross's life has been threatened, can you spare a man to spend a week, or two, or three, in the house?" Forget it. Even if such an outrageous request was granted, he could hear Harley trumpeting, "This mad agent of mine planted police in my house," and suing him blind.

Go for a visit, uninvited, and be taken sick, like Elizabeth? No, one invalid too many.

Call Harley and—? He did, Monday morning.

Voice offhand, he said, "Sometimes a change of place is

helpful, Harley, when you're stuck on page x. I have to go to Colorado for a convocation of publishers.'' (An invention; he could stay at a hotel. Or, shiny thought, with Elizabeth.) ''Could you use my apartment, do you think, for a week or so? The typewriter works.''

His apartment was above the parlor-floor offices in the house on Stuyvesant Square. Large, white, booklined, and comfortable. Harley had slept there several times after late parties.

Worrying slow, vague answer, as though Harley was thinking of something else. ''No . . . thanks. I've got to stay bolted down here until I work things out. Mustn't keep you . . . thanks anyway.''

EIGHTEEN

Jill's nonappearance on Monday rippled a number of small
ponds.

Her partner Daisy McCall, exhausted after a partying
weekend, waited hopefully for her and then began to simmer.
She had planned a quiet day in the back office, perhaps a little
rest on the batik-covered cot; let Jill shoulder what load there
was today, although Mondays were never busy. At ten-thirty,
she called and got no answer. Her private life, her Harley life,
was an open book to Daisy. The first thought that occurred to
her was that perhaps the two of them had gone off, and to hell
with Mrs. Harley Ross.

After a short hesitation, she dialed his number. "I'm trying
to track Jill down," she said to the unwelcoming grunt. "Have
you any idea where she is, instead of here, where she's supposed
to be?"

"No, but I had an impression she was in New York, some
antiques thing."

Maybe she told me and I just forgot, Daisy thought; I do
have my scatty moments. But then Mrs. Braine turned up, Mrs.
Walker Braine, one of their best customers, and demanded Jill.
"She promised me Thursday, absolutely promised, that this
morning she'd have swatched of silk velvet for that walnut
loveseat I bought. I most particularly wanted to get that settled."
No swatches were to be found in or around Jill's desk. Mrs.
Braine went off in a dangerous huff.

When Jill failed to turn up at twelve-fifteen for her appointment with Dr. Vintner, his receptionist was irritated and

perplexed. She was the only one of his roster who flatly refused to wait more than ten minutes for his attentions, and therefore had to be tightly scheduled. This took a great deal of thought and calculation on the receptionists's part. But Ms. Gaynor was one of Dr. Vintner's pet patients, and it had to be done. Late, and the shop right down the street—! Cancel her outright? No. She called, reluctantly, and was told, "Oh, dear. She may be in New York. Or maybe not." Cancel her.

Marta got up from a festive luncheon table in lenox, Massachusetts, thinking about Harley and how strange, congested, he had sounded yesterday. To banish a niggle that had persisted at the back of her mind, she called the Four Corners Shop in Brookfield Center and asked to speak to Jill Gaynor.

"Oh God, who'll be wanting her next?" a distracted Daisy cried. "I honestly haven't a clue where she is, maybe New York."

A man arrived at the Four Corners at three o'clock with a peach-gold small bundle in a basket: a six-weeks-old apricot poodle. "I arranged to bring him here at this time, I called Miss Gaynor Saturday, she said she didn't know where all she'd be over the weekend so bring him to the shop at three."

Eying the poodle doubtfully, and then enchantedly, Daisy asked, "Is he paid for? Or she?"

"He. No. A hundred and fifty dollars. His mother, Tompkins' Tralee, was a champion," said the poodle breeder Tompkins cannily.

"I'll—lets see—" Daisy touched the curly head, soft as cashmere, and looked into the sparkling, inquiring dark eyes. "I'll give you my check and then get it from her. Oh, *what* a darling."

She hoped her personal bank balance was up to it; she was at no time quite sure what the balance was, as she never filled in check stubs. But if by any outside chance the check bounced, Jill could make it good tomorrow. No, not tomorrow, her day off. Wednesday.

Demeter Klanavage, a composer of contemporary music, arrived at Jill's door at seven with wine, flowers, and well-defined intentions. He used the knocker, then the bell, then his impatient knuckles on the door. They had met at a party the week before and he had told her the instruments, the harmonies, she brought to his mind. "Come and dine next Monday at seven," she had said, "and tell me more." Splendid woman. But perhaps with no sense of time. Absentmindedly leaving his flowers and wine on the doorstep, he went in search of a public telephone to try her number.

No answer. Not such a splendid woman after all. Had she just forgotten? But women, Klanavage assured himself, do not forget *me*. Give her a half hour, and try again. She looked well worth it.

Seven-thirty to eight. Zero. Eight until nine. Nothing. Type *anything* to unfreeze the ice block, forget your head, let your fingers do it. Let's see, he's about to install Mina the barmaid in his dressing room, right next to his and Cissie's bedroom. . . . He saw his fingers striking letters and words began appearing on the sheet of yellow paper. Don't even, for a while, look at the paper, just at the keys.

He allowed himself a glance halfway down the page. The last six words he had typed were: "Harley, darling. It's been too long." He ripped the page out of the machine, only to have to retrieve it from the wastebasket to see if Jill had invaded the first and second paragraphs too.

She hadn't; but there was nothing worth saving anyway, not a word of it.

He got up and poured a fifth cup of coffee for which he had no earthly desire.

"This is an excellent way to go crazy," he said aloud. Would he now, always, type Jill back at himself? Would he hear Jill's name any time he heard *any* typewriter?

. . . It's been too long. Very long indeed, for Jill, up in the pine grove. Forever is too long, Harley darling.

"No, this is just a normal human reaction," he said. "Natural enough. After all, I'm only human. Tomorrow . . ."

Tomorrow and tomorrow and tomorrow creeps in this petty pace from day to day, to the last syllable of recorded time; and all our yesterdays have lighted fools the way to dusty death.

Ken Bliven had come, unnoticed, late to work at close to

ten o'clock. It was an unseasonably hot day for May, ninety degrees, and milky with humidity. He dug one hole and then with a cold bottle of ale took a rest. He was sweat-soaked, and felt himself exhausted and ill-treated. So okay, so he hadn't gotten to bed till five, this was still too bloody much.

Especially as . .. It was in the lean-to at the back of a ramshackle empty house down the street from his rented room at Ma Tyler's. An army blanket taken from his own bed covered it. Hid the glitter and power and blue and scarlet paintwork. He'd paint it yellow and green, two colors he'd always liked. File off the registration number. Crazy to leave a thing like that unattended, unchained, while you went in and sloshed down beer at Little Harry's Bar, well after midnight on Saturday.

He didn't ride off on it; he wheeled it for half a mile down lanes and back roads before he claimed for his own the saddle and the roar.

So why was he breaking his ass at this nothing job? Have another ale first, think it over, a hundred and twenty a week. More or less his own boss, the writer guy seemed to have lost interest in the whole thing. Time off when he wanted it— But then he remembered that woman, kicking him awake. She might come back up any time. Every day.

"I'll just sit on this nice rock and see what a good gardener you are, shall I?" Bitch.

Without even bothering to put a tree into the hole, he went down the path and knocked loudly at the back door. He peered through the window when his knock produced no response. The kitchen was empty. He tried the knob, by natural instinct slowly and silently. The door wasn't locked.

He went in and stood listening. The silence was interrupted by a sudden heavy crash. Following the noise to its source, he opened the workroom door.

Harley, who had just hurled his typewriter across the room with all his strength, went over and looked down at it. "You're no damned good to me but I'm sorry anyway," he said. "That did it. You're finished."

Crazy, Ken thought, he doesn't even know I'm here.

"Mr. Ross?"

The great blue bloodshot eyes turned to him without interest and it seemed without recognition.

"Fell on the floor," he said musingly. "Shame. I'll have to get a new one. Been a good friend."

Like he's talking about someone dead, crossed Ken's mind.

Harley went to his desk drawer, took out a bottle, and poured scotch into his coffee cup under the thirsty gaze of his visitor. He drank it all down, drew several long breaths, and said with an eerie briskness, "Well. What brings you here? Need more supplies or something? Running out of trees? Warm as it is, I think the geraniums could go in today. And the ageratum."

"I came to quit," Ken said. "It's breaking my back. Like coal mining or laying railroad tracks. Let's see, how much would you owe me, from nine to eleven?"

"But you can't," Harley said, and then gathering his wits, "I mean, you'll have to give me time to find someone else. The garden's going to be in magazines and newspapers—"

Magazines and newspapers were no part of Ken's world, which was made immediately evident by the blank face.

"One week," Harley said. "I'll give you a bonus of a hundred dollars in addition to your salary."

Ken had been no good at mathematics in school but his brain instantly supplied the figures: forty-four dollars a day. His dark eyes flickered and darted while he considered.

"Okay. One thing, Mr. Ross, would you ask Mrs. Ross to keep away from the place while I'm working? She slows me down, talking and all."

Nothing to do but swallow it; the insolence was after all no more than a pinprick following upon deep and terrible wounds. And his obvious malicious dislike of her might be a good thing.

"I'll try. Now hadn't you better get back to work?"

"I forgot my lunch, can I get something, cheese or something for a sandwich, from the kitchen?"

"Help yourself."

Ken carved four thick slices off a clove-studded half ham, found rye bread, noticed a cookie jar and pocketed six thin coconut-molasses cookies, and took two apples and a banana from a bowl of fruit on the kitchen table.

He decided, departing with this collation, that he would forget his lunch every day.

One week, Harley repeated mentally, hearing his own half command, half plea. Now where did I—? Then he remembered.

"After lunch," he said. "After lunch is time enough to buy a new typewriter." With his toe, he lightly touched the slaughtered machine on the floor. "And anyway, you were five years, five books, old."

He not only bought his typewriter, he did other errands after lunch. Probably unnecessary, but they gave him a pleasure in his secret efficiency, or wiliness.

From a special account of his own he had opened two days after Marta's return, he took three thousand dollars in cash.

He drove over to see Mike Heard, who would be leaving the following week to see to the London production of his play *Again Mrs. Withers*. They had several drinks and Harley asked casually if Mike woiuld let him have the keys to his cabin in Vermont—"if again Mrs. *Ross* gets a bit too much for me. I'm having a hell of a time with the book." Mike Heard, who was his oldest and closest friend, handed over the keys. "Feel free. I know how it is."

At the A&P, he bought three large bagfuls of canned goods and a dozen cartons of cigarettes. At Lavery's Beauty Saloon, he bought a large long curly blond wig. "My wife's head is about the size on mine," he explained to an eighteen-year-old clerk who was not literarily inclined and had no idea who he was. Trim the wig later. *If* any of this was ever wanted at all.

He left his purchases in the trunk of the car in the garage, brought down an armload of clothing and his passport, got a suitcase from the hall closet, and packed everything neatly.

He patted the suitcase lid before he closed and locked the trunk. "You're a nice little runaway kit," he murmured.

Must look normal—whatever *that* is—he thought, expecting Marta back sometime after dinner. He showered and shaved, a routine he had skipped in the morning, and put on English flannels and one of his Bean's gingham shirts, silky green and white. Too bad redblooded males couldn't wear makeup; it would be nice to cover up the gray, mottled look of his skin, and the lavender patches, all right, bags, under his eyes. Maybe dark glasses, say that his eyes were tired after all that work. But he never wore dark glasses in the house.

Normal. That was the word.

Oh dear, Mrs. Nairn thought, as she deposited a platter of curried shrimp and rice on the sideboard. What had happened to the briefly radiant man of Saturday morning? She had thought he'd turned some kind of corner and now everything was going to be all right.

"Shall I keep food hot for Mrs. Ross?" She had to ask it twice before he said, "She'll probably have eaten, but yes, just in case—" and rolled wine around in his glass.

Marta arrive at nine. With a long drive to New York ahead of them, the Faunts only stopped to say hello.

She looked blooming, cream and rose and gold. It had been a happy weekend. Sergius Dormer had taken a fancy to her and showed it opently and gallantly. Kitty Riddle had been amusing, and the Faunts were always good company. It had been, strange thing to admit, a relief to be away from Harley and his manic, unpredictable moods.

Still warm with the admiration of a rich, handsome, and extremely important man, she asked, dropping onto the sofa, "Did you miss me?"

Harley had arranged a little scene to indicate a quiet evening: the *Times* flopped over one arm of the wing chair, an open book face down, and a tall scotch and water on the table beside it.

He sat down. "I missed you terribly," he said. "Yes, I may truly say, terribly." There was no emotion of any kind in his voice.

"And did you get any work done?"

"Yes, some work. Done. Damned nuisance—the faithful old typewriter conked out and I had to get a new one this afternoon."

She would not, she would *not*, give up her glow, her feeling of being desirable to be near. Merrily she said, "We must swing a bottle of champagne against it for the christening."

Harley yawned and picked up his book. "I want to finish

this tonight and see if Glynn stays down there at the bottom of the barrell all the way through. Catch me up on your weekend tomorrow."

It might be a good idea, Marta thought, to make sure that everything was in order, as Mrs. Nairn had been dismissed for three days and Harley had the house to himself.

His bedroom was untidy, clothes everywhere, but that was to be expected. She dumped the overflowing ashtray beside the bed into the wastebasket. He had given up smoking in bed the year they were married. Dangerous, he said. She must have a word with him tomorrow, when he was in a more receptive mood.

His bathroom was too large to be untidied by a few damp trailing white towels and a slight disarray of bottles and jars on the long white marble counter that held the oval basin. Another ashtray filled to the brim. Reaching for it, she saw the slender little case and picked it up. Gold. Initials engraved on one corner: J. G. She opened it. Mascara, and a tiny folding brush.

Jill Gaynor, redoing her face after a bath in Harley's bathroom. And yes, there was a flush of beige pink on one of the towels, makeup rubbed off.

How careless of him. In every possible way.

She looked at her own taut face in the mirror where Jill had so recently gazed, brushing on her mascara. She dropped the gold case into the pocket of her rose linen suit, walked out onto the landing and stood very still at the top of the stairs.

No. Not now. He looked ill and unapproachable. Tomorrow. When they'd both be fresh and rested and fully ready for combat.

NINETEEN

Bad night, Harley reported to himself upon waking.

He had had one awful dream after another, dreams of surging black bottomless seas into which he had plunged from a high cliff and found himself fatally far from the surface; dreams of something around his neck, so that he couldn't breathe. One dream was so unendurable that in the middle of it another section of his brain came to the rescue and said, This is only a dream, wake up and it will be over. He did wake up, gasping, and smoke a cigarette.

The mirrored face of the dreamer terrified him when at seven he got up and thought about embarking on the day. Marta, just across the landing, in her bedroom. Marta, with her clear china-blue eyes, the whites immaculate. Not a bright woman, but she knew him too well, could read his face, his skin, his eyes, his mouth. For all he knew she could see into his head, and hear his mind turning over.

Must have some recovery time, before the eyes took their measure of him.

He locked the bedroom door, an act he had never had occasion to do before in this house, and went back to bed. There was a light knock at nine.

"Harley?" The knell. He pulled the covers closer around him and called blurrily, "Didn't get any sleep . . . indigestion. Later . . ."

"I must talk to you. It's important to say the least."

"For God's sake let me sleep, I was just drifting off—"

He had a frightful vision of her getting the ladder out of the

131

garage and leaning it against the house wall and climbing in at the window to get at him.

"Why have you locked your door?"

"Go away." And then remembering the invisible loaded gun in her hand, he broke into a sweat and said, "Please, darling. See you at lunch."

He's hiding, Marta thought. Maybe when he went up to bed he noticed that the little gold case had disappeared, although about trifles he was not usually a noticing man.

She considered strategy, over her breakfast of sautéed chicken livers and drippingly ripe mango.

Her own juices were busy in her veins. She got into her car and drove through the green and blue and crystal morning to Brookfield Center, where she found a parking place half a block down from the Four Corners Shop.

She entered in a decisive manner, to the tune of a silver dinner bell hung on the lavender front door. The large room inside, half dusk, half sunlight celebrating glitter and color and sheen, was empty. From somewhere in back a voice called anxiously, "Jill?"

That would be Jill's addleheaded partner. She emerged, carrying an apricot poodle puppy, and seeing Marta commandingly facing her said, "Oh, sorry, I thought—"

"You read my mind," Marta said. "I want Jill Gaynor too."

"Today's her day off, but—I'm afraid you can't reach her at home, she's not there, at least she didn't answer, three times in a row—I've thought and thought, and it couldn't be the Antiques Fair, that doesn't start until next week. Oh dear, listening to me unloading my worries when I . . . Is there anything I can help you with, were you interested in buying something?"

Silences from people can be frightening, Daisy had been thinking when the silver bell rang. Especially from Jill, who was never silent, her presence and perfume and clothes talking even when she was saying nothing at all. Where *was* Jill? In her autocratic way, she was reliable. She was professional. She was there when you expected her to be there.

There had been her own nice Aunt Belinda, who called her from London every Christmas, until on one Christmas there was a silence. Daisy investigated, transatlantically and expensively. Her Aunt Belinda had died on Christmas Eve. But what a silly thought. And her aunt had been eighty-three.

"I suppose you might try her house, she may not be answering her phone for some reason," she said to Marta.

There was no response to the banging of the door knocker at the brick house. Jill's small dark blue Mercedes stood at the curb in front of it. Marta touched the hood. Cold. Eyes could be watching her from above, dark eyes, amused.

A man in a blue coverall came out of the arch in the brick wall beside the house. Complainingly, he said to Marta as though making use of the nearest ear, stranger or not, "And where's her laundry? She always leaves it outside her garden door if she's not at home when I come. No sign of it."

Not bothering to reply, Marta went and got into her car and drove home. Without any hesitation, she walked into Harley's workroom and found him standing looking out of a window, shoulders humpingly dropped forward.

"So you finally gathered the strength to get up."

He didn't immediately turn around. "I kept thinking of coffee and I couldn't stand it so—"

He thought he could face her now, for a little while. He had resorted to another long hot shower and the forgotten eye drops from Rome that gave his eyes a temporary clear blue sparkle.

She held out the gold case on the flat of her palm. "Jill's. It was in your bathroom. I thought I'd ask her why but I couldn't find her, at the shop or at home."

Adopting the vagueness of the innocent, he said, "She stopped by on Sunday for a drink on her way to New York. Redid her face, I suppose, before she left. People do use bathrooms even in other people's houses, you know."

"That partner of hers seems not to know where she is and is acting like an untied bundle," Marta said; not at all in any concern for Jill. "She isn't to be found apparently, even by her laundryman."

She paused, watching him closely. "Are you sure you don't have her tucked away, out of sight? For your own greater convenience?"

A hoarse, "For God's *sake*, Marta—"

"Are you sure?"

Her eyes were two swords piercing him. He was just barely able to make himself move past her, out into the hall. Over his shoulder; he said, "Work to do in the garden. I'll see you later on."

The cold leashed-in rage of the night and the morning boiled over. The words followed him down the hall. "If you haven't got her put away somewhere—If I were a friend of hers I might start to worry. A road accident or something . . ."

Tredbloom of Filmways called John the same morning. He was a man of one- and two-word sentences, occasionally allowing himself the extravagance of three or four words in a row.

"Board meeting. Bankers. Schedule. Upcomings. Blockbuster. A must. About Nero and Noreen? Or whatever it is?"

"Cissie and Caeser, Well, *what* about it? I thought you were all aseethe."

"I am. Terrific. Climax. Especially. Two chapters of that needed. To knock them out. Wrap it up. In between? Doesn't matter."

A rather trying task for a writer; but on the other hand it might be a heaven-sent project. Keep Harley's hands off his wife's throat, fingers otherwise occupied.

If it was true at all; hard to believe on a gleaming May morning. And not just one of Harley's personal, passing storms.

He called Mute and got Mrs. Nairn. "Must talk to Harley. Important. Sorry." God, Tredbloom was catching; he hastened to retrieve his own natural style. "How is Dove, by the way, before I crash into the workroom morning?"

"Very well, thank you. Enjoying your books." Which was not quite true. Dove had been curiously reluctant to return, after their three days away. She was always, in Mrs. Nairn's words, a biddable child, but she had turned stubborn and then pleading, her gray eyes very wide and darkened as though in sudden cloud-shadow. "Can't I stay here for another week? I don't want to go back there yet."

Deal firmly with her fear. There were two mouths to be fed. It would take a good deal of time to find a job as good as this one had been, until Mrs. Ross. "Are you mad, Dove?" she asked mildly. "Custard about to kitten, to say nothing of school?"

To Harley, John reported his conversation with Tredbloom. ". . . so as he points out through a cloud of cigar smoke the whole thing could be wrapped up at their board meeting three weeks from today. It's a hell of a thing to ask you to do but—"

In a drowned faraway voice, Harley said, "I'll try."

At lunch, Marta said, "What a greaty ugly machine that new one is, although it must have cost a fortune." Underminingly, searching for the sorest place of all, "I did like the Olivetti. I wonder whether this new one knows how to write Harley Ross novels?"

He thought he'd make a stab at, well, beginning to *think* about the last chapters, after lunch. Passing the living room, he heard her talking to somone on the telephone.

"Fascinating . . . Jill Gaynor seems to have disappeared, at least temporarily. Oh, hadn't you heard? . . . Yes, if you hear anything, do let me know. And vice versa of course."

Once Marta started on any track or trail, she continued forward, he knew; a singleminded woman. She would not be satisfied to let Jill, inexplicably, drop out, through some mysterious hole in her private world.

She would pursue the matter.

Think about other things this afternoon. Think about the last chapters tomorrow morning. (Odd conjunction of disparate ideas: *the last chapters*.) There had been a high wind the night before, when a cool dry weather front sailed down from Canada and swept away the humid heat. The wind probably hadn't done anything to his blanket of pine needles, that deep in the grove. But it wouldn't hurt to check. He had checked yesterday, and that time for no reason at all.

Ken Bliven, languidly setting out geraniums—at least it was a change from those godawful trees—saw him climbing the meadow slope. He noted and filed away his impression that his employer was oddly stooping, head hanging. Normally he stood up straight. This was the second day in a row he'd gone up the meadow and vanished into the woods. What was the big deal up there in the woods? Or maybe he was just nutty about the smell of pine trees?

Twinkles of sun sifted their way down through the dark heavy branches and made a butterfly flicker over the warm brown covering of pine needles, peaceful and undisturbed by last night's wind.

Marta at lunch. Greedily downing crepes filled with sherried creamed chicken and relishing her Chablis. Marta, who had murdered Jill. "Pass the pepper grinder . . . and I might like a touch more wine."

Must shake off the feeling of obsession with Jill, standing here by her grave, thinking too much about her, letting her get in the way of other matters. In a way, in a terrible way, Jill was beside the point. A cruel epitaph. But must stick to the main point. Marta.

Three weeks. One week for any services he would require of Ken Bliven. Then two weeks to do two chapters.

Salvation, Harley thought. I'll be given myself back, and my future, whole. Well, almost. But only if. And when.

TWENTY

Marta threw herself heartily and maliciously into the sport of finding out where Jill Gaynor was.

She called Lee Pierson, a real estate agent and a good friend, and asked if she'd sold or rented any attractive places in or around Mute in the past three weeks or so. If such a nest existed, it would probably be nearby; long drives, long absences would be awkward for Harley to explain. And it was impossible to imagine Jill holed up in a rented room or motel, awaiting his pleasure.

"Sadly enough I haven't," Lee said.

"Well, you all know each other's business, what about your colleagues, or rivals?"

"Not much is moving, of course it's late in the season, and we all had a fabulous spring. I'll call around and ask if you like."

Next she looked into the checkbook to see if he had recently noted down any substantial sum. This hunt was barren. The check for two hundred and fifty dollars to self was habitual; Harley liked having plenty of cash on hand.

Of course, she reminded herself, she had no way of knowing what other accounts he might have. She must make a point—like any good and sensible wife—to request that he lay his, their, finances before her, bring her up to date on the figures. How much in stock, how much in hand, and more importantly how much in toto.

Nice timing. Lee called back just as the workroom door

137

opened. "I have a few bits and pieces for you—but what's it all about?"

"My mother's thinking of buying something near us and I want to see what kind of place is going for what kind of money now that the gold-mine season is over."

The footsteps, which had started up the stairs, paused. Harley came back down.

"You're not serious. You know you couldn't live within twenty-five miles of that bitch."

"It's as good a way as any to find out what's going on in real estate in Mute and environs," Marta said, her message unmistakable. *Are you sure you don't have her tucked away, out of sight?*

She spent a pleasant afternoon pursuing her investigations along the dappled roads under the radiant trees of May. A little Swiss-looking chalet in a thicket of alders at the top of a high hill seemed ideal: safe and secret and very pretty. She had her trespassing excuse ready. She was looking for the Ingersolls, perhaps she had the wrong address? The front door opened and a small towheaded boy came out, followed by a golden Labrador retriever. No go.

Instinctively she knew that Jill wouldn't settle for the fake colonial or the ranch house suburban; in any case, there were very few houses of that sort in Mute. Which left her only two more to study: a handsome converted barn in a meadow full of daisies, and a romantic octagonal gray clapboard house with white shutters and for no reason at all a widow's walk on the roof.

At the barn, her knock brought an enraged woman obviously in the middle of the process of dying her hair. It hung in dripping Medusa snake tendrils around her stained face. "For God's sake, I thought it was United Parcel or I wouldn't have answered at all," she said.

The gray and white house was apparently occupied but at the moment seemed empty. She looked in at the windows, and saw hunting prints, a rack of guns on the wall, a bottle of Usher's Scotch on a table, a Harris tweed topcoat thrown over a chair. Of course, Jill could have taken it furnished, but its visual message was entirely male.

"What the hell do you think you're doing?" a voice demanded close behind her.

"I was told the Ingersolls live here and I couldn't get an answer to my knock—"

He studied her from head to foot, sun on her buttery hair and on a rose and creamy cheek. "Let's try it again. You know and *I'll* answer."

"Thank you so much," Marta said blandly. "Wrong address, but such a pretty house."

Harley was fixing drinks when she got home. Making his voice deliberately tense, anxious, he asked, "Any luck? In your reconnaissance for . . . your mother?"

"No luck. Were there any calls for me? And oh, has Jill turned up yet?"

"You seem to be more interested in her than I am, at the moment," Harley said; this time the tone weary, resigned. He handed her her drink and lifted his own glass. "Considering my somewhat sterile day"—clinking the glass to hers—"here's to nobody and nothing."

This is becoming an obsession, John thought. One of two. Harley and Elizabeth Ross. After all, he had other pressing matters requiring his attention.

Elizabeth wasn't home at seven, or eight-thirty, or ten minutes after nine. He gave in to the other obsession, telling himself that Rome might be burning while he resisted it. Normally, he would have committed his information to paper. A great deal of money was involved; but this was a matter of course in the handling of the works of Harley Ross.

He called Mute at nine-thirty and got Marta. *Still breathing, anyway.* It was easier to take if you made a fantasy out of it. "He's outside somewhere—I'll see if I can find him."

She found him. Harley said irritably, "You're getting to be almost a nuisance, John. What is it this time?"

"I thought you'd like to know you've fallen into another barrel of gold. Mackie in Australia—the biggest and best paperback house—wants all five books and of course the sixth when it's ready. Any luck yet?"

The paperback information seemed to have fallen on deaf

ears. "For Christ's sake, leave me alone, will you? I—have—only—one—week." Five words, emphatic, desperate.

One week? He had three weeks. Correct him? Or let it go, let him race against the tighter deadline, maybe it would supply the necessary adrenalin. Uncertain and troubled, he let it go.

I have only one week. For what?

Elizabeth was home at ten.

"I thought our understanding was that you had more or less settled down, at least socially speaking."

"I have. I was innocently occupied on a videotape commercial. Safflower oil, to be exact."

"Today's Tuesday," he informed her. "I can't tomorrow—can you leave early Thursday afternoon and come up with me to stay a night or so at the Mute Arms? *In* the McIndoe arms, or part of the time?"

"Is there anything *new* wrong?" But the huskily tired voice smiled at him.

"I don't know. But please allow me my Gaelic premonitions—something pricking at my thumbs and I don't think at my age it's arthritis."

"Whatever you say, John darling," Elizabeth answered, sounding as if she meant it entirely, and for good.

Wednesdays, Mrs. Asa Green cleaned Jill Gaynor's house. She was much treasured by her employers because she worked hard, neither drank nor smoke, and was honest as the day. Her one addiction was television, preferably crime or violence or both; the bloodier the better.

She was not surprised at nine to find the house empty. Miss Gaynor (Mrs. Green spurned the usage of Ms. as misleading and possibly immoral) off to work a bit early. She was surprised at not finding her twenty dollars on the mantlepiece. Such an oversight, in this house, had never come her way before.

She was interrupted in her cleaning by three telephone calls. The first was from Miss Gaynor's partner, wanting to know if Jill was there. "No, Mrs. McCall, I thought she was at work. . . ." She was tempted to add that it was funny, no money had been left, but mustn't let her tongue rattle about private matters.

"Oh, dear," Daisy said, and thought that the words were rapidly becoming her anthem. "People have been calling here— her dressmaker, she missed a fitting last evening, and some man who said his name was Demeter Klanavage, but I must have it wrong, it doesn't sound— They'll probably be calling her at home. Not that she's there, you say."

The dressmaker did call, and shortly afterward there was a man's voice on the line, foreign-sounding. "Not at home," Mrs. Green said briskly to him; you had to take a firm hand with foreigners.

The voice somehow put her in mind of the man she had seen banging away at Miss Gaynor's door when she had passed on her way to the A&P Monday evening. Nasty black beard on him. Mrs. Green equated beards with dark deeds.

In a state between fascination and worry, her head swarming with images from the television screen, beatings, stranglings, shootings, burnings, she went up to the bedroom and checked the luggage on the closet shelf. All there, including the small alligator overnight case. She went down to the mailbox and found it jammed full.

Could that bearded man have—done something to her and just now called to see if anybody had discovered his crime? Murderers returning to the scene . . . by telephone at least. . . .

She thought of Harley Ross. She disapproved of his association with Miss Gaynor, but he was a fact of life, Miss Gaynor's life. He'd know if anybody would.

She found his number in the telephone book. A woman answered. The housekeeper? Not by nature a giver or receiver of gossip, Mrs. Green if she had heard about the return of Mrs. Ross had forgotten it.

"Sorry, he's not here. Any message?"

"This is Mrs. Green. I clean for Miss Gaynor. I just wanted to ask him if he knows where she is, people are calling here, and she's not at work. If he does will you please ask him to call me back?" The voice said yes, she would.

Scalded, Marta carefully replaced the receiver instead of crashing it down as she wanted to, and stared ahead of her not seeing anything, but hearing the behind-the-back voices, perhaps trimmed with laughter.

Jill Gaynor's *cleaning woman* expecting Harley to know where Jill was, at any and all times. Has she herself turned into Mute's prime current joke? Was some kind of bedroom farce being played by the two of them, to the enjoyment of their friends? "It's too killing, Marta with her embroidery and her invitations, lady of the manor again. . . ."

Her invitations. Mouth hard, she dialed the number. No, they couldn't make it tonight, but yes, tomorrow night would be fun, what a wonderful idea to celebrate Harley's new almost-movie. And how was he?"

"Not *very* manic," Marta said, and added, "and up to any number of projects." Which could read: I know all about Jill, see how calm and unworried I am?

She kept the little plan in her pocket until Harley came out of his room for his lunchtime drinks. She had no idea what he did there, mornings, now. There wasn't a sound from his new typewriter, and he very seldom worked in longhand. "It just jumps out of my head onto the keys," he would say. "I simply put a quarter into the slot and the torrent turns itself on."

She intended, first and foremost, instant punishment, in the form of hard reminding knuckle-rapping. And then a little tight-rope-walking verbal teasing, with the Hydes there. Maybe something about looking over a possible house for her mother, on Broken Saddle Road . . .

"Gin and tonic for me, it's getting hot. I was talking to Alison this morning . . ." She paused, waiting for her drink.

Back turned to her, "How is she?"

"Fine. I asked them to dinner tomorrow night. Just the two of them." She took a sip of her drink and looked up into his eyes. "Just the four of us. For once, we can really *talk*. Won't that be nice?"

TWENTY-ONE

Won't that be nice?

Won't *what* be nice? What was she going to do to him, in her smiling fury over Jill?

It would have to be an academic question.

He couldn't sleep, after going to bed at midnight, although he took a sleeping pill and two aspirins. He *had* to be rested, he had to be ready, for the most important and worst day of his life. Lie still, if you can't sleep. Don't toss, thrash, sweat.

Marta ticking away across the landing, the time set . . . or was it the primer? Up goes Harley Ross in flame and smoke, flesh and bones consumed, nothing left but ashes.

But, with her help, I've already gotten there all by myself, Harley thought. A pile of ashes, to powder to nothing at the touch of a fingertip . . .

His pendulum swung. Somewhere about three o'clock, he found his mind surging with ideas for his last two chapters.

Danger and death . . . a strange and powerful stimulus.

He got up at seven and showered for five minutes. The ablutions of the priest preparing for the sacrifice, he thought, soaping himself, letting the brisk water, first hot and then cold, tingle on his face, which felt stiff as a marble mask.

And how (official notebook and pencil at the ready) did Mr. Ross spend that day? Oh, just as always, Sergeant. Into his workroom at seven-thirty, typewriter going on like mad, a midmorning check on his garden . . . everthing was just as usual, until—

He selected a bound copy of *A Thunder of Eagles* from the

bookcase and began, thunderously, typing again the first page. By God, this reads well, he thought. It's still fresh. It's still pretty terrific. On the other side of a broad, deep chasm, this blazing exhilaration was waiting for him, to be tasted and delighted in again.

He stopped to drink a cup of coffee and went back to his typing. At ten o'clock, he called Perdita Twinn. If this was a novel of his, she would be a subplot. Useful as filler, diversion; providing a denser texture of interest.

"Perdita, could you kill two birds with one stone for me? I have a novella I want typed—seventy pages or so—and I want you to test my new machine in the course of it and see if you think it measures up. I'm not quite satisfied with the touch."

"Yes, certainly, what time, Mr. Ross?"

"About three forty-five, will that suit you?"

She had a church guild meeting at three and an invitation to tea with the rector at four. "That suits me perfectly, Mr. Ross," she said without a moment's pause.

"If there's no one there, the door will be unlocked, I'll leave everything ready for you on the desk."

He dug out a manuscript for Perdita he had never been satisfied with, written nights when he was still up to his neck in advertising. One day, he had thought, he might expand it into a book, but so far he hadn't needed it. Not with all those ideas he used to have, a new book shaping in his head when he was three quarters of the way through his current one.

At twenty after ten, he went up the path to the anniversary garden.

It was a cool, dark day under heavy cloud, the kind of day May often offers just before the shine of June. Snowball weather, an aunt of his had called it; the last lick of cold, just when the snowball bushes were blooming.

Quite by coincidence, he found Ken Bliven working, raking white pebbles around a circular path. His heavy black vinyl jacket was tossed on the ground, near an empty ale bottle.

"Glad to find you here," Harley said. "I didn't hear your motorcycle this morning."

"That's only a borrowed one. Couldn't get it today so I had myself dropped off." His face came as close as it could to beaming. Eyes flickering, he said, "I practically have one of my own right now. Secondhand—it needs a bit of fixing up."

"Leave the pebbles for a while. There's a little tree up in the woods I want transplanted—"

"Jeez, Mr. Ross," Ken interrupted peevishly, "all I need is another tree."

"A redbud," Harley said enthusiastically. "Sometimes called a Judas tree. It gets pink flowers on it before the leaves open. This one's quite small. If it turns out to have a deep root system, I'll help. We'll take the dolly and a spade for each of us."

So that's the big deal up in the woods, Ken thought. More trees to break my ass with. Oh well, hell, it was Thursday, only one more day, one hundred dollars on top of his salary. Not used to offering any kind of compliance or cooperation, he said, "Gotta have an ale first, I'm dry."

"Go ahead." Harley stood, hands in his pockets, watching him drink it. His blue, steady, burning gaze made Ken nervous and he drank faster than he wanted to, coughing through the large final gulp.

They walked in silence up the tilted meadow, Ken dragging the dolly with the spades behind him. The outer circle of the woods, mostly oak and sycamore, was in new heavy leaf and the day was even darker underneath. Harley felt his companion rebelliously lagging. "It's not far now. Next those pines you can see up ahead."

A moment later, he pointed to a comely small tree about three feet high. Actually it was a larch, but Ken would never know the difference. It was the right size, in the right place.

With a put-upon sigh, Ken took one of the spades from the dolly.

"First cut the earth with it in a circle about a foot away from the tree," Harley ordered. "Then we'll both dig."

Ken put one foot to the spade edge and drove it into the soft ground. Harley picked up the other spade and swung it, swift, hard, and audibly crushing, against the back of the shiny dark bent head.

There wasn't even a cry. Ken fell forward, over the tree, and then toppled sideways to the ground and lay there face down, blood and brains, red and gray, the white of bone, visible through the rapidly drenching hair.

Harley looked first to see if any blood had splashed on the dolly. No, it was clean, in its bright yellow paint, three feet away from the body.

He took Ken by the ankles and dragged him over last year's leaves and needles to the blanket of pine needles. He went back, picked up the bloodied spade, took a folded tarpaulin off the dolly—big, black, heavy, rubber-coated, a tarpaulin that meant business—and covered the body and the spade with it.

Then, very carefully, he checked the little rough path the dragged body had made, and kicked and scattered the leaves so that there wasn't any sign of blood, or of the passage of any human thing.

It was reassuring, going down the meadow with the dolly, to see that the tracks made by it on the way up were already almost obliterated; the long grass, clovered and daisied, was young and bouyant, lifting itself up with its own green juices.

He could have been alone in the world, on top of the bluff. It was invisible from the house. But his hands were shaking, now, as he picked up the black vinyl jacket from the ground. He put the scarlet morocco wallet into one pocket and the envelopes with their left-handed block-lettered addresses into the other.

He went close to the edge of the bluff, where there was a ten-foot perimeter of long soft grass between it and the garden. He lay down, rolled, kicked the earth with his feet, dug several clumps loose with his hands, rolled again, gouged a deep dent with one heel. Then he got up and brushed himself off.

Step number one disposed of. Step number—what?—three to be taken care of tonight. Late.

At lunch, Marta said, "I thought spatchcock chicken for tonight. I have it in my Cordon Bleu cookbook. Mrs. Nairn says she'll have no trouble at all with it."

She rolled a strawberry in sugar and put it into her mouth. "All sorts of delicious things in the sauce, shallots and sherry and French mustard. And then it's served with watercress and lemon fingers. Oh, and straw potatoes."

Harley had asked for a cup of beef bullion after his silent consumption of three martinis. He said, "That sounds good," and with an effort of will picked up his cup and drank down the contents.

"I had thought, first, brains in black butter but I'm not sure Ormond likes brains, some people don't."

Harley reached for his coffee, hesitated, then got up and went and got a bottle and poured brandy into it. Watching him steadily, Marta said, "You've developed a tremor in your hands. You really must watch your drinking. And to go off on another subject—" She sugared a second strawberry. "Tomorrow we'll have a financial session. You really must bring me up to date on what we have and where we stand. It's only common sense. If anything should happen to you I'd be all at sea—I mean as far as business matters go."

"Oh," Harley said suddenly, "between your chicken spatchcock and your banking conference it slipped my mind. Ev Morse called me yesterday morning, you were out and I forgot to tell you. She's coming up this afternoon with a photographer. Your garden is scheduled for October and to make the deadline they've got to shoot today."

Marta looked startled but pleased. "For God's sake, Harley, on this short notice—and it's not finished anyway last I looked— "

"They'll shoot the finished portions. Anything can be done with the right man at the camera. Now, let's see, what will you wear?"

"Mmmmm—there's the new geranium red—or the ivory raw silk trousers suit . . ."

"Ivory suits you beautifully," Harley said, voice animated, color back, startlingly bright, on cheeks that had been green-pale. "Good stage set for your coloring."

Lightly Marta said, "It's nice to have you taking an interest in me again, Harley."

He looked at his watch. "One-ten. Plenty of time for a nap if you like—you'll look even better. They'll be here around four. We'll go up first and find some attractive backgrounds for you so there won't be a lot of milling around when they get here."

"But this nasty gray day, and it may rain—"

"You can't argue with publishing deadlines. Colors photograph better in diffused light anyway, and if it does rain—umbrellas, slickers, it could be charming. Dramatic, offbeat. His eyes glittered.

Shortly before three he knocked at Mrs. Nairn's bedroom door. When, covering a yawn, she opened it, he said apologetically, "I hope I didn't wake you?"

"No, just reading."

"I wonder if you would do a great favor for me. You know gardens. Will you go to Phelps' Nursery and pick me out, oh, enough pretty things to fill a space roughly ten feet by ten? They have individual ones in those little pots now. If you could go soon, my layabout up there can at least get some of them in before he leaves. I'd go myself but—"

He needed no excuse. Mrs. Nairn put up a polite palm. "I enjoy spending other people's money. Let's see, the Hydes won't be here until six-thirty, dinner at eight-thirty—no problem."

A day of tight timing indeed; of schedules that must be met.

He forgot all about Dove.

Going down the stairway to the kitchen at a little before three, Mrs. Nairn saw his car backing out of the garage. She went out to her own car with the pleasant prospect of being extravagant; Harley had given her a blank check.

He drove east and west, then north on Prince's Road, which ran along the far end of his ten acres. He pulled the car onto the grass and under a tree, not far from the gate in the long split-rail fence. Nice to have a nothing-looking car; anybody's car.

At a speed just under a run, he went through the woods and the meadow, down the path and into the house. Standing in the hall, recovering his breath, he called, "Ready, Marta?"

TWENTY-TWO

Dove was hard put to it to concentrate on her school day. At some time the night before—"dead of night, naturally," Mrs. Nairn said—Custard had had her kittens, in a cardboard box in Mrs. Nairn's closet. "I helped her along a bit, everything's fine, all of them alive and squirming," was the report when Dove slipped into her room at six o'clock.

An anxiety that had haunted her in her sleep and twisted her dreams surfaced. "Someone at school yesterday said if my cat had kittens they'd be . . . drowned?" There was early woe in the gray eyes.

"Stuff and nonsense," her aunt said. "We'll keep one and your Aunt Grace is a whiz at placing animals. She'll want to keep one for herself. But not for a while."

Reprieved and grateful, Dove studied ways in which to thank Aunt Em. Flowers, she loved wild flowers. A great big bunch of pink clover, and daisies, and shootingstars, and honeysuckle. They were thick, now, in the upper meadow.

When the school bus dropped her at twenty after three, she allowed herself a brief visit to the kittens, then took off her good plaid cotton suit and pretty red shoes and changed to sandals and her lavender gingham, now officially an old dress.

She ran down the back stairs and out the kitchen door. Lighthearted and brimming over with various happinesses, the kittens, the flowers, the dark gray adventurous windy air, she went up the steep path. Her head was level with the top of the bluff when through the birch branches she saw them.

149

It was a picture that remained forever sharp in every detail, a photograph never to be forgotten or erased.

Mrs. Ross in ivory long pants an a tunic, her hair shining strangely in the gray light like the gold paint on statues in church, smiling, holding a trowel in one hand. Harley, studying her, head cocked. Then, ''Turn around facing the edge. I want to see how the view looks beyond you. Spectacular, I should think. Maybe we can get the house roof and a bit of the waterfall.''

His wife walked, straight and graceful, to within two feet of the lip. Harley sprang. The motion of his arm was a blur but for Dove his hand was eternally placed on Mrs. Ross's back, just above the waist.

She flew into the air like a great creamy bird. And then from below, fifty feet down, there was a crashing and crumpling kind of noise on the slate terrace. Somewhere in the flight a scream had happened.

Unable to move, unwilling to grasp, to even think, what had just happened, Dove saw Harley, after only a second's stillness, turn and run, not straight up the meadow but into the alders at one side of it. Running, running, running away—

Running, running, her own feet down the path, stumbling, falling, skinning her knee, up again, gasping and moaning, not with her own pain, which she hardly felt. Through the apple orchard, and then— Don't, don't, look to the left at the slate terrace, there's nothing there, it didn't happen, but don't look anyway.

Tears of shock and terror now half blinding her, she ran around to the front of the house and in at the door.

Run. Up the stairs, along the hall. *Where* was Aunt Em? Her hands without being aware of the order from her brain locked the door. Don't look out the window. The terrace is right underneath. There's nothing there but don't. Don't make this funny noise, and don't cry, because he might come back.

Clicking sound, what was that? Her teeth chattering, as though it was winter and she'd been out skating too long. She went into the bathroom and bit hard on a towel to stop it. Passing at least six feet away from the windows, looking straight in front of her, she flung herself face down on her bed. Bury her head in the pillow, bury it in darkness, when it was dark you couldn't see things, but you could hear things. The scream, torn flying sound. The thumping crash.

Her room was filled with the terrible noises, bouncing off the walls and striking her again and again.

She lifted her head, reached an arm under her pillow, and found the butterfly card with John McIndoe's number in it. But she couldn't call him, she couldn't leave her room, she couldn't unlock the door.

An exhaustion she had never known came over her. She sighed, turned over on her side, drew her knees up to her chest, and fell into a desperate and profound sleep.

Perdita Twinn was cherishing the lovely feeling of possession, however temporary, in Harley's workroom. *His* desk. *His* chair. *His* typewriter. Even the smell of him, tobacco, faintly, and an edge of clean sharp lavender.

She typed twenty pages at her high steady speed. Nothing wrong with this machine; typing on it, Perdita thought, is like riding in a Rolls-Royce, or rather as she imagined such a feeling to be. Odd, delightful, to have the house, the silent house, *his* house to herself. It was, just for this little while, as if she lived here. With *him*.

Shortly after four, she became aware of thirst and thought that probably nobody would mind if she got herself some milk or fruit juice from the refrigerator. In reality her little journey to the kitchen was to relish his floor underfoot, his walls around her.

She paused, wondering if the rain had started yet, and on her way to the refrigerator looked out one of the big windows.

She saw, perhaps six feet from the trees around the waterfall pool, the stilled, tangled heap of ivory and scarlet on the slate, upon which the first few drops were gently pattering.

With a noise boiling up in her throat, trying to tear its way out, she backed away from the window. Then she fainted. As she fell, her forehead hit the sharp corner of the sill and blood poured down her face.

Her faint lasted slightly longer than three minutes. She wondered what she was doing on the floor, remembered, got up whimpering to herself, and felt as if she was going to faint again when she heard her own voice, in church, crying out "Kill Mrs. Ross."

There could be no question that that . . . heap was any longer alive. Anyway, no power on earth woiuld ever make her look at it again.

Kill Mrs. Ross. And she, Perdita, was alone in the house with her there outside, or what had once been her.

Panic sent her into the workroom, where she gathered up her bag and fled to her car. She had turned from the drive into the road when she saw her face, blood streaming from her forehead, in the mirror. Blood as red as the blood on the slates.

The stained face began to shake. Oh, what shall I do? My fingerprints will be all over the typewriter keys—

I had a headache, officer. I get these bad headaches. Touch of migraine, really. I always have to lie down in a darkened room with eau de cologne sprinkled over a handkerchief on my forehead. No, I saw and heard nothing before I left. . . .

Mrs. Nairn's car, coming in the opposite direction, heading home, passed her. Mrs. Nairn was startled and concerned to see the bloodied face and honked her horn and would have stopped but Perdita's car increased its speed to the point of danger on the narrow twisting road. Oh well, on her way to her doctor probably, she couldn't drive at all if she was really badly hurt. . . .

Perdita reached her house, put the car in the garage, and went in at the back door. Upstairs, fast, pull the blinds, shake out the 4711 cologne, but first wash her face, cover up the wound with a bandage—

Her scene set, she lay on her bed, eyes closed, breath gaspingly hard to maintain; silently, trying to pray, waiting for the knock on the door. Waiting for the great shining knife to drop from above and sever her head, there on the block.

It was four-ten when Mrs. Nairn entered the house. She went directly into the kitchen, leaving the eight cardboard boxes of plants in the back seat and trunk of her car for that Bliven boy to unpack.

While not behind schedule, she liked to have things well in hand, dinner guests expected; the senator and his wife had never dined there before, and just the two of them at that. She got well started on her salad, peeled Belgian endive of its faintly flawed outer leaves and set it in water to chill; washed and trimmed the plump white mushrooms and put them in their bowl of olive oil and thyme; opened a can of tiny anchovy fillets.

Dove must be upstairs reading. Those books of Mr. McIndoe's were like a tent sheltered in for comfort. Never too early to become a Jane Austen addict, though.

Filling the pepper grinder at the kitchen table, she glanced out the window. A handful of Malabar peppercorns fell to the floor with a whispering rattle.

"Dear God," Mrs. Nairn said. "Oh, dear God."

Going out the back door and over to Mrs. Ross was one of the hardest things she had ever had to do in her life. The blue eyes were open, staring at the sky. She bent and without any kind of hope felt for a pulse. Poor, ghastly, broken Marta Ross. In compassion, and for decency, she went inside and got a dark blanket and covered the body with it. Then she went to the telephone and called the police.

"Dead?" Chief Bello said. "Are you sure?"

"Yes. Must have fallen over the edge of the bluff, or God knows what. . . ."

Chief Bello knew at once this was going to be too much for him. He hadn't the technical squad, he hadn't the men. He called state police headquarters.

The town police arrived a four-thirty, the state police five minutes later, and Harley a minute and a half after the siren was cut off, in the drive.

Mrs. Nairn was waiting for him at the door. She put a strong hand on his arm. "Trouble," she said, and told him. And then, "Don't go out, don't look. There are police with her and more of them up on the bluff. You'll want brandy—"

"Marta," he said in a soft low voice. Then his voice grew louder until the house rang and rocked with her name. "Marta! *Marta!"*

His hands were over his face now. Tears trickled around the outer edges of them.

"Come sit down. Living room. Brandy by your chair. They'll want to talk to you, you must get hold of yourself. I'll sit with you until they come back. Come now, here's the glass, I'll hold it for you."

"No, I'll . . ." He reached out an uncertain hand for the glass, not bothering to wipe away his tears, which, brimming, running, made his eyes look even more enormous. "You, too."

"I will indeed," Mrs. Nairn said, and poured herself a stiff tot.

Up on the bluff, while the technical men were at work on the terrace, Lieutenant Glenn of the state police, with Chief Bello at his side for courtesy's sake, read the signs of struggle in the gouged grass near the edge. He shouted below for one of the two men with cameras, and then turned his attention to the black vinyl jacket near his foot. He pulled an expensive scarlet wallet out of the pocket and went through it.

"Hers," he said. He was large, albino-fair, and a man of few words.

On the back of the jacket, in nailheads, were emblazoned two-foot-high initials: K. B.

"And in this pocket we find—" Glen held out some dirtily fingered envelopes with block-printed addresses.

"I know that kid," Bello said, excited to be able to make a major contribution. "Rotten lousy kid, nothing but trouble since he was twelve, I *heard* Mr. Ross had hired him to do garden work— We have four more of those crazy notes down at the station right now."

A panting sergeant with a camera arrived. The scuffled grass was photographed, and the jacket, and the wallet, outside and in.

"He'll probably," Bello said, "be miles away by now. In a stolen car likely or not. Can you send out a—"

The alarm was radioed from Glenn's car, the description accurately supplied by Bello, "I know you can't use this," he added, "but he's got a head like a—like a sort of snake. He lives in Ma Tyler's boarding house, I'll sent one of my men to check there. But like I say he's probably at least halfway to the next county."

The house seemed to be teeming with men, although there

were only five troopers and three town policemen. Mrs. Nairn was still sitting protectively by Harley on the sofa. He had had a second brandy and sat rigid.

Pushed, smashed, from the very garden you built her up there, Bello thought, looking at the destroyed face.

In a flat low voice, Harley answered questions about Ken Bliven. He'd been going to quit at the end of the week, he said, and then, his voice going up a note, "He muttered something about not liking Mrs. Ross and would she please stay away while he was working—"

"He liked her well enough to try something, in the grass," remarked a trooper named Skiff, and got a murderous glance from Glenn.

"Perdita," Harley said suddenly. "Where is she? She was supposed to be here typing something for me—"

Glenn followed him into the workroom. Typewriter uncovered, scrawled-over yellow sheets on the desk to the right of it, cleanly typed white manuscript to the left. "She *was* here, then."

In a few halting but well-chosen words he explained Perdita, for Glenn. "She was to come in midafternoon. She's never let me down yet, and you can see she didn't this time. But she's never left a job unfinished yet either, not even if it took her till morning. The most loyal, reliable . . . I wonder what made her—"

From the doorway, Mrs. Nairn said a little unwillingly, "She drove past me the other way when I was coming back to the house. Blood on her face, I was a bit worried about her, although it may be . . ." Her voice trailed off.

Glenn sent a trooper to Perdita Twinn's house.

The knock when it came was even worse than she had imagined, sounding through her little house.

Her scheme fell apart. She was to be *seen*, prone with her migraine, and the scent of cologne chilling the air. But someone had to let the man *in*.

She had expected some alarmingly strong and big and official young man, fate in a uniform. Instead, in the doorway, she saw a man in his fifties, tubby, rosy, something vaguely familiar about the eyes—

"Why, Petey," the man said. "I remember Twinn but I somehow didn't connect the name up right. It must be thirty-five years. . . . ''

Cutting across her terror, a memory came back, a schoolyard, where a girl had been hitting and kicking her and a boy with nice brown eyes had pried the girl away. She had been Petey at school until, when?—twelve, when her mother heard the nickname and banished it.

She burst into the end of her planned explanation instead of the careful beginning.

"But I *didn't,*" she cried. "I didn't do it. I don't know how to kill anything."

Sergeant Billstone had been transferred from Mute to New Haven when he was in his thirties and—with his phenomenal memory for faces, facts, and figures—looked promising. He was too basically kind, and worried about people, and tending to see their side of things, to be a successful policeman. More transfers, same rung or a little way down, Bridgeport, Mystic, Stonington, and home to Mute. Along the way he had lost a pale, tired, disappointed wife.

Perdita in some fashion remind him of her, although her hair was still dark, and she was not as thin. She might be quite— well, yes—if she wasn't so obviously terrified.

In a manner unbefitting a state policeman, he said, "Suppose you get yourself a nice hot cup of tea, and put my name in the pot. Then we'll have a chat."

Over the tea, at the kitchen table, curiously comforted and unafraid now, Perdita said with intelligent clarity:

"I was typing there, in the workroom. I went to the kitchen for some milk and I saw her. I fainted and cut my forehead against the kitchen windowsill. If you look you may find the blood still there on the sharp corner. It was so awful that I just—waked up and ran away."

"Don't blame you," he said, remembering all too vividly. "But why didn't you call the police—Petey?"

Hands clenched in her lap, looking down, she said, "I suppose a lot of people are afraid of the police."

Watching her lashes, and eating the buttered homemade bread she had placed before him, he said in a forward-looking way,

"No need to be afraid of the police, Perdita. I guess at our ages I should call you that now."

"Just for the record, Mr. Ross, where were you this afternoon?" Glenn asked.

"I left the house just before Mrs. Nairn did, I saw her car in my mirror. About three, Mrs. Nairn?"

After Marta, he had run through the covers of the alders and into the woods, across the far meadow and through the gate in the fence to his car.

"I walk in the afternoons when I'm writing." Glenn knew this to be true; he had read in the Mute *Observer* an account of the famous writer's workday. "I drove to the reservoir and walked around it, it's a good four miles I suppose."

A rattle of hard rain from the east hit the windowpanes.

"Yes, a least four miles. . . ." The big drained voice going vague. "Is she . . . covered?"

"She's just leaving," Glenn said, and almost bit his tongue for it. The siren started up outside. "Why they think they need that commotion now—"

He wished Ross would wipe away the tear streaks down his face. Taking notes in shorthand, he cast a sharp eye at the other man's hands. Struggle, grass stains, earth dirt, probably flesh scratched away— The nails were large ovaled squares, immaculate.

Returning to Ken Bliven, Harley said, "More or less a lazy good-for-nothing, but you can't get help these days. And you keep feeling that maybe there's something you can do about these kids." Wearily hospitable, he asked, "Drinks for anyone?" and got because of Glenn's presence reluctant refusals. "Then a pot of hot coffee, Mrs. Nairn, if you will."

The coffee was consumed. The roomful of men left, Glenn saying casually to Harley, "You'll be here if and when we need you in the next few days?"

"Of course."

In the silence left behind, Mrs. Nairn said in a sudden startled way, "But where is Dove?"

"Dove?" Harley stared at her and then gave his head a bemused shake.

She was more puzzled and mildly concerned than actually worried; she was still caught up in the overwhelming fact of Marta Ross's dreadful death.

"She might have stopped off at someone's house on the way home from school. She's usually good about calling in to report but of course no one was here. Or rather . . ."

"Yes," Harley said grimly, standing by the window, "Marta was here. For a while."

"Or—could she be in her room, maybe hiding God knows, scared to death, her windows look right on the terrace?" Voice rising now.

Harley forestalled her. "Good Christ, a car turning in at the drive, more police? You get the door. I'll go up and see if she's there."

TWENTY-THREE

"We'll be arriving in time for early drinks," John said, looking at his watch as they drove through the town center. "Cheering thought on a rainy afternoon."

He had picked up an ambivalent Elizabeth in front of the great bronze soar of the Seagram building on Park Avenue, where her agency was. Her skin and eyes shone at him, but her mouth corners were delicately down and her brown worried.

She wore a mysteriously cut dress of violet-colored silk linen and a white-belled scent of lilies of the valley. "You look, if pensive, marvelous," he said, after a quick hello kiss, and told her in a few sentences why his thumbs were still pricking.

"It's trying," Elizabeth said, "feeling two or three things at once. *You*. It's a long time since Sunday. But then, where we're going, and why." She paused, and then as if continuing an interrupted mental sequence to herself, ". . . it's like those antique movie serials at the Museum of Modern Art. But I don't know which of them, Harley or Marta, is tied to the railroad tracks and I don't really want to be around when the train runs over one of them."

He left her to her troubled silence and as the miles ran away under his wheels thought how comfortable it was, circumstances notwithstanding, that neither of them felt compelled to offer the other a penny for their thoughts.

After the turnoff north of Danbury, he caught her smiling to herself and said, "What about?"

"This time, just you."

He stopped the car for three minutes and then with a sigh

turned the ignition key. "The big bad world getting in the way of us just when the curtain's going up. Oh well—sooner or later— "

It was five minutes to five when he turned in to the driveway and stopped the car beside the house. Even in the rainy gloom, he was instantly disturbed by the evidence of his eyes, the roweled flung gravel, the sense of wheels, brakes, in frantic haste.

Maybe just a social converging, a late lunch party, although on Thursday, Harley with hard work to get through—?

Mrs. Nairn answered the door. Her face, her gray pallor, offered bad news before she opened her mouth. "Come in. I'm glad you're here. Mrs. Ross is dead. The police have just left."

In the hall, she filled in the details. John, listening in stunned silence, had a feeling of *dèjà vu*. Was it only Tuesday when he had said to himself, half mocking, *She's still breathing, anyway?*

"Where is he?" Elizabeth asked whitely. "Lying down, or—"

Mrs. Nairn turned and looked up the stairs. "My head is all whichways. He went up just a minute or so ago to see if Dove was there, in her room. Maybe she isn't there, but at a friend's house, which was my first thought—but maybe—although I wouldn't think, the rain—maybe he's gone out looking for her, the poor man is half out of his mind."

"You don't know where Dove was, this afternoon, then?" The question from John was very quiet.

"No. I was out on an errand, and when I came back . . ." She couldn't repeat it, call up the vision again. "Oh, God. This on top of everything else. I'll try calling a couple of numbers."

"And if he's half out of his mind, I'd better go out and look for him," John said.

Something about his voice made Elizabeth say, "I'll go with you."

"No. You will not." The order was explicit and unanswerable. "Stay with Mrs. Nairn, you'd just be in the way, you're not dressed for tramping around in the rain."

"You can borrow one of Mr. Ross's raincoats, Mr. McIndoe,

I'll just run up and get it for you—"

"Thanks, I have one in the car. We'll probably be back in no time."

Leaving the house, he gave in without hesitation to the terrible urgency. He hadn't the slightest doubt that one way or another Harley was responsible for Marta's death. Dove's voice: "People being expendable." The Bliven kid, hired to work on Harley's garden, a known troublemaker to say the least, according to Mrs. Nairn. And, "The names he called her, the words he used, when she came back . . . he was crying . . . and saying by God he wouldn't have it."

John was a man of penetrating and when necessity pressed almost clairvoyant intelligence. He listened for a second or two to the voices.

"He went up just a minute or so ago to see if Dove was there . . . maybe he's gone out looking for her." A search for a witness, taking him out into the inhospitable evening?

The Ross property in front, between the house and the road, was shallow, perhaps two hundred feet. Now if I were Dove, running, wanting to hide, I wouldn't want headlights spiking me, showing me, to anyone behind me. I'd choose the distances of woods and meadows behind the house . . . that is, if panic allowed clear choice.

A tossup, but he turned and began to run around the house to the back.

It was the siren that woke Dove, a wild floating banner of distress. She lay cold and shivering, face down on her bed, head buried in the crook of her elbow. Recollection came flooding back. Don't go to the window—

In a way, the hard rain against the panes was comforting. It hid whatever noises there might be in the house below. Aunt Em might not be back. He might be there. Just the two of them, alone.

There was no clock in the room and she had no idea of the time. She was too frightened to turn on the lamp. He might be watching from outside. To see if anyone was upstairs. In a room that looked down on the terrace.

After a time, she heard a little sound at the door. In the gray

gloom, she saw the knob very quietly turning. Not Aunt Em,
she would have called cheerily, "Dove?"

Another slow turning of the knob and then a little testing,
jerking noise. He'd know if the door was locked that there
must be someone inside. He knew this was her room.

"Dove?" he said. Not the reverberating voice she was used
to; but low, so she hardly heard it.

She got up off her bed and went to the nearest window.
Kenniston kept the windows well oiled. It went up silently.
The screens didn't go on until Memorial Day. She got up on
the sill, turned around, grasped the sill with both hands and
dropped herself over.

The ball of her sandaled foot found the extended wooden
frame of the kitchen window underneath. At the same time she
flung herself sideways and just managed to grasp with one
hand, rapidly joined by the other, the gray painted metal spout
running down the house two feet to her right. The spout was
wet and when she took her foot from the window frame and
let her hands take all her weight she slipped rather than made
her way to the ground, landing on her feet with an impact that
sent shock up through her body to pound her head. She saw a
tear in the skin across one palm, blood fiercely beginning.

Running up the path in the rain, she thought she could hear
Aunt Em, "Rust. Lockjaw. We'll get the iodine immediately."

The rain and wind beat her hair into her eyes and the wet
squelching sandals impeded her. Each plunging step drove her
toes hard into the sandals, but she couldn't stop to take them
off. Anyway, snakes, brambles, nameless jagged things underfoot—

All he had to do when nobody came to the locked door was
to go into Aunt Em's room and throw open the window and
lean out and see her own window, open. That would take only
a second, and by now he might be close, after her, a towering
tall man with great strong racing running legs, he'd go down
the back stairway, out the kitchen door. What if, just behind
her, any minute now, he called her name in that same soft,
low way.

"Dove?"

No, she hadn't heard it, she hadn't, it was all in her head.

Dove, rustled the aspen tree she ran under, *Dove*, whispered the long grass catching at her knees.

She had no clear idea of what he might do to her if he caught her. He was all the fear, all the horror that could be contained in this dim rainy world. He had the bad roaring giant out of long-ago, half-forgotten fairy tales.

Instinctively, she headed for the darkness, the shelter of the woods. There was no safe lighted place to run *to*, there was only, now, invisibility. If he didn't know where she was, if he didn't see her gingham dress, he couldn't do anything to her until . . .

Until when? Until what? Who besides him would know where to look for her, know she was in the woods? She could hear in her head, over her gasping tears, Aunt Em, in the open kitchen door, calling out into the rain, "Dove? *Dove!*"

"Dove . . ." A half shout, she had no idea from where, behind or to the left or right of her, echoing through the tall rain-sighing trees.

The drive to survival of any trapped terrified thing, however small and young, directed her to stop her blind run. And listen. And let her ears tell her how and where to move. Facing in one direction she thought that voice hadn't come from, she flattened and narrowed herself against the hole of an enormous pine.

The place where she stood trembling was charcoal dark. Far up ahead she could see a ghostly deep gray green where the trees were thinner. Stay here, in the dark. If she couldn't see him he couldn't see her. She wondered if you could hear a person's heart beating if you were a few feet away. She wanted to cry, to moan, but fastened her lips hard against her teeth.

A sense of disaster took her, as only the forthright naked mind of a child can envision it. The things you couldn't stop happening. The wild flail of a hand across her face last year, from an enraged English teacher, when, reciting aloud Milton's "On His Blindness" she had lost it helplessly in the middle. The absence of her father, who couldn't come until July. No matter what. The death of her aunt's beloved springer spaniel Alice. Aunt Em had tried to stop it with love and medicine, but it couldn't be stopped. Kittens, other people's kittens, thrown into the water to bubble their tiny lives away. . . .

But disaster could at least be put off. A little time snatched, and then a little more.

There was a faint crunch on the ground. A groping hand touched her shoulder in the dark. Now the screams came, pouring from her throat as she ran. She shot through a slender opening between two trees, too narrow to allow the passage of anyone large, made a wild half-circle to her right, still screaming. She tripped over something lumpy and slippery, rubber, wet, and fell onto what in her panic felt like a shoulder and an arm beneath.

Strong hands lifted her up. Her eyes, used not to the darkness, looked up into the face of fear, of doom, just barely sketched and perhaps partly seen from memory. Although the great eyes seemed to glow by themselves, in another light of their own.

He held her by the upper arms, which he had pinned against her sides. His grip hurt.

He said, "What shall I do with you? What, Dove? You shouldn't have been home, you know, when . . . you really shouldn't have . . ."

Dove managed a whispered torn *"Oh please . . ."*

"Everything was done, everything was taken care of. Everything worked. Except you. Did you," carefully, "see it all?"

The shrinking of the shoulders under his hands answered him. Or gave him a second answer after the screams of mortal terror when he had first touched her.

Again he said in an exhaused, puzzled way, "What . . . shall I do with you?"

"The first thing you can do is let her go, Harley," a voice said directly behind him.

She felt, as well as heard, the grunt or groan that seemed to run all the way through Harley's body. Then the great twitch of the flesh.

There was a rustle of cloth and John flicked on his lighter, holding a strange flame-lit hand over it to shield it from the rain.

"Just to see how we stand," he explained. A civilized bookish man, he had no weapons. He hadn't thought about a knife from the kitchen, or a heavy stick picked up along the way. Not even the knee, to use, with Dove between them. He moved a little closer, not to Harley but to her, to let her feel some kind of warmth, some possibility of a nightmare's end. He stepped on a foot, under what the lighter showed to be tarpaulin sprawled on the ground, clumsily outlining the shape of a body.

"Who is this I've just stepped on?" For Dove, he had to keep it level, conversational, although he thought he'd strangle getting the question out.

"Not someone who can be of any assistance to you. He's dead. And anyway, beside the point," Harley said. He picked up Dove and held her sideways across him, legs and arms pinioned.

"I've only to swing her, once, against this tree, the neck—"

"What are your terms?" John asked, still with remote calm.

"Six hours."

John wanted to tell him he'd never get away, twenty-four, forty-eight hours wouldn't be enough for him, or a week, or a month. But a Harley brought face to face with despair and his arrival at the end of things was something he didn't want to happen to Dove; who would then no longer be of any use to him. And who had, from what he had said, seen him in the act of killing Marta.

In a judicious manner, he lowered the lighter to his left wrist. "Five-twenty. All right, eleven-twenty."

Harley hesitated. "But how can I be sure that—"

He looked down at Dove, who was now unable to make a sound of any sort, and who knew in her shrinking bones that her life was in some delicate balance.

"*. . . the neck . . .*"

"I promise," John said slowly and quietly. "Poor citizenship on my part, no doubt, but nothing they can do to you will ever bring Marta, and whoever this is"—although he was quiet sure it was the expendable boy—"back to life."

"All right." Harley threw Dove at him, bent to his left and, John realized later, as a form of extra insurance, swung a heavy fallen length of pine branch against the dark wet head.

The blow knocked him out, prone, clear of the tarpaulin.

After a time a voice from far away entered his darkness. ''Mr. McIndoe, Mr. McIndoe,'' a low wailing. His head was in her lap.

He put a hand to the side of his head, felt what was certainly blood, rolled over onto his knees and got to his feet. He reached down for her hand. ''We're both going to be an awful mess when we get home, safe, which will be in a few short minutes.''

He had no idea where his lighter had flown, but better this way, she wouldn't see him, lifting the corner of the tarpaulin, reaching in an arm, finding a wrist, cold, its pulse silenced.

Then, straightening himself up as a pain began to hammer in his head, he said, ''Can you, for my sake and yours, not say a word about what happened here, until tomorrow?''

It seemed an impossible thing to ask of a ten-year-old child.

Dove, who had thought he was dead, her dear Mr. McIndoe, said just above a whisper, ''Well, you promised. Yes, I promise.''

''You were in the woods looking for—what?''

She tried to maker her mind work. ''Catnip for Custard?''

Mrs. Nairn and Elizabeth were waiting for them at the open, golden kitchen door. From fifteen feet away, he called, ''Don't anybody scream at the sight of us. Dove's fine, she's got my blood on her, I'm fine too except that in the dark I stumbled and hit my head on a tree branch.''

Neither did scream, but a great healing pour of concern and love and care warmed them and brought them back into the world of light, of sanity, with walls and doors and windows around it.

''But where,'' Mrs. Nairn asked, expertly bandaging John's head while Elizabeth, tears on her cheeks, handed him a cup of strong hot tea, ''—shallow wound I'd say but I'll call the doctor anyway—where is Mr. Ross?''

Simultaneously, Elizabeth's, ''I'd make it scotch but they say that after a head wound—'' and John's, ''I haven't the faintest idea where Harley is. Thank you kindly, Elizabeth.''

''Now then, Dove, we'll go and get you washed up and into something clean and there'll be food for everybody. What *were* you up to, by the way?''

The hazed and now helpless gray eyes went to John's bandage. "I—" But the words wouldn't come out. He saved her the lie. "Catnip for Custard," he said.

Mrs. Nairn didn't believe a word of it, but she saw that Dove looked like someone recovering, very slowly, from a dangerous brink of illness. Reaction to something, she didn't know what, was settling in.

"Or better still, milk toast and bed for you. Right now. In my room, I think. You can say good night to the kittens. I know where there's catnip, we'll get some tomorrow."

"If you'll stay by her side until eleven-thirty," John murmured close to Mrs. Nairn's ear.

Unquestioning she said, "I will. Oh—can one of you call the Hydes and tell them not to come to dinner? And why?"

TWENTY-FOUR

He promised, Harley thought, walking around the house to the front, getting into his car, starting the engine, turning down the drive, all the way on eggshells that might turn into dynamite that could blow him to hell.

He promised.

Elizabeth, in the living room with John, said, "That car—could that have been Harley?"

"I'll give you my opinion on the matter in a little under six hours," John said. "Come back here to me."

Harley drove steadily north. Thank God for the runaway kit, which he hadn't thought he'd need, safely stowed in the trunk.

Tensed all the way for the sirens of betrayal, he reached Pride's Crossings at the Massachusetts-Vermont border, drove another fifteen miles through the heavy rain, and took a narrow asphalted road to the left, up into the Green Mountains. After half a mile it became a dirt lane just wide enough for two cars to pass.

What if Mike Heard had hospitably distributed other keys? The long redwood cabin, large, porched, handsome in a rough-and-ready way, was reassuringly dark in its Norway spruces. He put the car in the garage behind the house, got out the heavy suitcase, and let himself in at the back door.

Don't cower. Be bold and at home. There's no way they can find you here, not when you've finished transforming yourself. He turned on the kitchen light, pushed open the pantry door, and saw to his pleasure and relief loaded shelves; and a case of whiskey on the floor. The food he'd brought would have lasted him for a week, but here was a whole bright future of sustenance.

Week after week, the police search for Harley Ross yielded nothing. As three of his five books had international settings, Interpol joined in the hunt; England, Italy, France.

Mike Heard, in London, read about the missing murdering best-selling novelist in the *Times*. Harley, and the keys to the cabin— Just one in a hundred possibilities, though. A man who could plot a book like Harley could would have any number of disappearing tricks up his sleeve. And he himself wouldn't want to be shooting anything in Vermont till fall. The hell with them, he thought. I'm on your side, you poor bastard. He had had severe trouble with both of his own wives. But you're on your own, Harley, if you're holed up there, can't get myself labeled accessory after the fact. And that Bliven boy (to quiet a not very active conscience)—nobody really knew by whose hand he had died, his record sounded as if he'd been asking for it.

It was conjectured over Mute drinks that Jill might be with Joe Grundy, who had left his Mirabelle and gone off to Cairo.

Harley gave himself a week to start a beard and get used to his tousled soft fair wig and his large gold-rimmed dark amber glasses.

He lived the life of any bohemian guest of Mike Heard's. He swam for a few aching minutes every morning in the icy lake below the house, smoked, read, selecting his books from copious shelves. He drank when he felt like it and as much as he felt like, slept heavily at night, ate with consuming hunger. And, he thought as the week drew to an end, got himself back.

On a Monday morning, he waked at seven, two hours earlier than now usual. Ritually, he drank orange juice, frozen, not fresh, but a small detail. He ate two pieces of toast. He made coffee and carried it to the table by the window which over-looked the lane approaching the cabin. The typewriter was a poor thing, a portable, old, manual, sticky; but that was another detail to be dismissed.

Let's see, where had he been, in *Cissie and Caesar?*

Shock ran through him. He didn't have the first chapters, they were back in his workroom in Mute, and the carbons were in John McIndoe's office in New York.

And he couldn't write it anyway. Harley Ross could not submit a Harley Ross novel to anyone.

Was he, after all, around some bend? Of no return? I've got to, he thought, I've got to write, it's what this, those deaths, was all about. His head buzzed with words wanting to burst out and hurl themselves onto the waiting yellow paper.

But what tale were they to tell?

Appalling, unthinkable, that there was nothing to write about. Because, if there wasn't, there would be nothing left, nothing at all.

But yes, there was.

Fresh from the mint, and a story that only he, Harley Ross, in all the world, could tell.

"Write about what you know, Harley," advised his English teacher, materializing out of the past, when he had been fourteen. He could see even now the fascinating mole on the end of her nose.

At eight-fifteen, unaware of his joyful savage grin, he began at high speed what was to be his headline-crashing and most sensationally successful book by far: *Diary of a Murderer*.

He finished it in five weeks and mailed it to John McIndoe. The short businesslike note accompanying the manuscript ended: "Promise me you'll try to get this into print. I've had nothing else to do, and now, nowhere else to go."